THE MARY JANE MISSION

Also by Daniel Wyatt

Two Wings and a Prayer
Maximum Effort
The Last Flight of the Arrow
The Mary Jane Mission
The Cotton Run
Pennant Man
Route 66

"The Falcon File" series:
The Fuehrermaster
The Filberg Consortium
Foo Fighters

THE MARY JANE MISSION

Daniel Wyatt

Published by
Bladud Books

Prologue

If the radiance of a thousand suns
Were to burn at once in the sky,
That would be like the splendor of the Mighty One...
I am become death—the destroyer of the worlds.

the ancient Sanskrit writings of the Mahabharata

GUAM—AUGUST 1945

Under the searing heat of the afternoon sun, two armed military policemen lingered by a navy jeep exchanging glances. For the last two hours they had been guarding a spot along a gravel roadway inside the fenced-in compound at Agana Naval Air Base. Flanking both sides of the road stretched solid jungle growth that was nearly as tall as a six-foot man. Jutting through the growth, ninety feet directly behind them, stood a silvery B-29 Superfortress bomber, her tail section dominating the tropical landscape like an old windmill on a deserted prairie farm.

The taller guard broke the silence, leaning the back of his legs against the jeep's tires, the machine gun resting by his leg. "Man, sure the hell is hot today!"

The other guard nodded in agreement, looking to the bomber. "Still can't figure it. Why are we guarding that thing, anyway? Who's going to steal it?"

"Ah, nobody, of course. The captain told us to not let anyone near it. That's all."

The shorter guard licked his dry lips. "I could sure handle a cold beer right now."

"Hell, yeah. You and me both."

"Hey, snap up, here comes somebody." The guard groped for his machine gun.

"Huh?"

"Over there."

A jeep raced towards them, kicking up a cloud of dust. Two men inside. The machine skidded to a halt opposite the MPs, who were now standing at stiff attention. Out hopped an army air force colonel and a navy captain.

"There she be, Colonel Cameron." The chubby captain thumbed at the bomber. "You wanna take a closer look at her?"

The trim, square-jawed colonel stared purposefully at the navy man. "You bet I do. Let's go." Cameron gawked at the two sweaty MPs as he walked past them. He and the captain pushed and tugged through the jungle without uttering a word, only the occasional grunt of exertion. Cameron arrived at the bomber first, just under the giant port wing. He welcomed the shade. He stopped and inspected the B-29. It was from the special bomber group, of which he was the commanding officer. The markings confirmed it—the large R inside the circle on the tail, the painting of a redhead woman in a tight, green, one-piece bathing suit and the name MARY JANE in black block letters below the cockpit port window.

"How did it get here, is what I want to know? It's one of yours, isn't it?"

The colonel was too preoccupied to answer at first. "She's one of mine, all right," he finally answered. He studied the wing for any damage. "But as far as how it got here. . . I don't have a damn clue."

"It's weird there was no sign of damage to the aircraft," the navy captain observed, frowning. "There aren't even any flattened trees behind her tail. Looks. . . I guess. . . like a forced landing. What do you think, colonel?"

"Hell if I know."

"The landing gear is intact. How could it have made a wheels-down landing in this mess of crap and brush. And. . . where are the crew?"

Colonel Cameron didn't know how to reply. He couldn't. Nothing made sense. Shaking his head, he climbed through the open nose hatch while the captain waited outside. Cameron found the front cabin deathly hot and stifling. First, he checked the navigator's station on the port side. No sign of the flight log. *Good.* He hoped that no one else had found it. He inspected the cockpit next. Hanging down from the fuselage, directly above the port seat, were two clean rags stuffed into two side-by-side bullet holes. The colonel pulled the rags out, examined them, then shoved his fingers through the holes. It seemed to him that the bomber must have been under enemy attack while in flight and that someone must have pushed rags into the bullet holes to keep the cabin pressure intact.

Next, he glanced down at the deck, where he saw dark stains. Blood spots? He squatted lower. Yeah. Blood spots. No mistake. He took a look around. Behind him, leading into the next aft compartment, more stains, only these were long and parallel, as if a person had dragged himself across the deck. The streaks ended abruptly at the opening to the bomb bay hatch, a few feet up from the deck. The colonel slowly opened the circular hatch door. Total darkness inside. He turned to catch the captain pulling himself up through the hole below.

"Is that blood?" the captain asked, bounding onto the deck.

"Yeah. Sure is. You see a flashlight anywhere?"

The captain spun around and checked the cockpit. "No, sir."

"Try the flight engineer's station. . . on the right."

"Got it. Here you are, colonel."

"Thanks." The colonel took the flashlight and flicked it on, and the navy officer peered over his shoulder. Cameron examined the bomb bay from nose to tail. The payload was gone, but more blood stains. "*Geez.*"

Looking aft, Cameron stepped onto the ladder and crawled into the tunnel over the bomb bay. He came out in what once was the gunners' compartment on earlier B-29s. No guns or sights here on this machine. Only bare metal fuselage. Nothing out of the ordinary. Walking on through the next bulkhead, he saw that the radar room had been left in order. Every piece of equipment in place. He strolled to the tail gun section where he found a box camera on the deck below the gun sight. He picked it up. The body was marked and scratched. The back was open and bent. The film gone. He set the camera down.

Crawling back through the tunnel, he stepped down to the deck and took another intrigued look at the blood streaks. He bent down on one knee and pushed his officer's cap back on his head. He was feeling the heat, but not as much as the overweight captain, who was sweating heavily.

"This is spooky, captain. Really spooky."

The captain tugged at his collar several times as if it were a fan to cool him off. "I'll say. It gives me the willies. Once the sun came up, there she was. You didn't hear anything?"

"Not a thing. No crash. No engines. Nothing."

Cameron rose and strode again into the cockpit for one last look at the bloodstains. Maybe he had it all wrong. Maybe the stains started in the bomb bay and ended in the cockpit. Then he dropped to the deck until his knees touched metal. He saw two more rags stuffed into the fuselage, this time on the right side near the intercom jack box. And. . . he caught sight of another item, a pair of glasses under the starboard seat. Reaching down and picking them up, he noted they were custom-made. Very thick. The metal rims were bent and one of the lenses cracked.

"What do you want done with your bomber, colonel?" the captain called out from near the nose hatch. "We're waiting on your orders."

Cameron stood. He slowly, casually, slid a hand into his pocket, still holding the glasses with the other hand. "I'll get someone down from North Field to pull it out. We'll look after it." Then he walked to the front hatch.

"By the way, I've been wondering about that. What is it?"

"What?"

"That." The captain looked down, pointing at a set of long, thick wires connected to a metal box about the size of a small bookshelf.

Cameron pondered that for a while, then turned to the navy officer, and replied as cordially as he could. "For your own good, pretend you never saw it."

"Got yuh."

One

GUAM—JULY 1990

Lieutenant Les Shilling opened his locker and appraised his flight equipment. He was going to *work*. But this was no normal nine-to-five job.

He began his routine by pulling on his G-suit, which he jokingly called his eighteen-hour girdle. He breathed in and zipped up the side. Then he sucked in his belly, held his breath, and bent down in order to zip up the leggings. Next, he threw on his chest harness and strapped the leg restraints on his calves. After that came the survival vest. He checked for his emergency items. *Strobe light. Water bottle. Knife. Flare gun. Smoke signal. . .* He placed them all on his body. Somewhere. A pocket here. A pocket there. He reached for his gloves and oxygen mask.

Last but not least, he grabbed his helmet. He was now ready to do battle, if called upon, in the way he was trained. He was an aerial gladiator, in much the same tradition as the coliseum combatants in the days of the old Roman Empire, but now acted out in the technical, computerized times of the late twentieth century.

Les turned a sharp left and lined up his F-18 Hornet fighter to the edge of the runway. The stream of white light from his wing sliced the heavy night air. He stopped and ran through the final checks before takeoff. He fidgeted in his seat until he felt as comfortable as any pilot could be in his G-suit, helmet, and oxygen mask. He took one last glance around the cockpit. So tight in such a self-contained space.

His high-tech enclosure—full of screens, digits, and dials—winked codes in bright colors. *Greens, yellows, whites.* Three large cathode-ray tubes measuring five inches square dominated the cockpit. These were the Digital Display Indicators. DDIs, as they were known in the business. The left and right DDIs exhibited precise three-color information for such items as radar navigation, weapons, sensor data, and system checks. The bottom screen was a Multipurpose Color Display—MPCD—that contained navigational data and a digitally-generated colored moving map. At eye level. . . the HUD. The Head-Up Display was an electro-optical instrument that superimposed numerical information onto the pilot's twelve-o'clock field of view. Les's cockpit was right out of *Star Wars*.

Finished with the final push-buttoning prior to flight, he readied himself for takeoff, gloved hand on the stick.

A voice crackled on his radio. "ZULU TWO-FOUR-THREE CLEARED FOR TAKEOFF. MAINTAIN RUNWAY HEADING AND CONTACT DEPARTURE CONTROL ON THREE-THREE-THREE DECIMAL THREE WHEN SAFELY AIRBORNE."

Les answered the tower with a prompt, "ROGER BARKSIDE."

Brakes on, he nudged the dual throttles forward to full military power. The roar of the engines, nearly 16,000 pounds of static thrust each, made him tingle, as it always did. He could hear the blast and felt the vibration through the cockpit Plexiglas and his padded helmet. Then he let go of the brakes. With two fingers of his left hand on the throttles, he lit the afterburners. The equivalent of one swift kick in the butt, and he was off and down the runway, gathering speed.

The acceleration was smooth and swift. With the stick in the neutral position and using the nose wheel steering button on the column, Les controlled the takeoff roll. He gently brought the stick back so that the angle of attack read *seven degrees* nose-up on the HUD. Then. . . in a blink, he was in the air. Before the far edge of the runway the wheels sucked into the belly with a slight jar. The HUD data changed from *gear down* to *gear up*. Over the water now he turned north, leaving Agana Naval Air Station and the tropical island of Guam behind him. He glanced at the HUD. Airspeed—*373 knots*. Altitude—*500 feet*. It was a half-moon night, no turbulence in the air, the silhouette of clouds ahead. He changed radio frequencies.

"BARKSIDE, ZULU TWO-FOUR-THREE AIRBORNE."

"ROGER ZULU TWO-FOUR-THREE, THIS IS BARKSIDE. TARGET TO PORT

ON HEADING THREE-FIVE-ZERO. ANGELS ONE. SPEED 200 KNOTS. RANGE ONE-THREE-ZERO."

Les came off afterburners, climbed and leveled off. His right hand went for the right DDI. Using the push buttons, he selected the proper functions for the Range While Search—RWS—mode which detected targets out to eighty nautical miles. The DDI glowed brightly with symbols and bits of info. But no target. He tapped the decrease range and azimuth buttons to obtain the required range. In a short time, he saw the lights of Tinian below. His MPCD verified it. He recognized the Manhattan-shaped island on the color display.

Then a target appeared.

The Single Target Track—the STT—mode burned a prompt onto the HUD. A flick of a switch on the stick, he changed the air-to-air mode from RWS to STT. Now he could track a single target with more clarity, as well as be ready for steering commands and shoot prompts for the armed missiles he was carrying on the wing tips and fuselage.

"ZULU TWO-FOUR-THREE. TARGET SHOULD BE DEAD AHEAD. RANGE TEN MILES."

Les hit the radio button. "ROGER BARKSIDE. I SEE IT."

"ZULU TWO-FOUR-THREE, GO BUTTON ONE-FOUR LEFT."

"ROGER." Les's gloved hand reached to his up-front control at chest level and changed the radio frequency from the right radio to the left radio. The comm 1 channel display window confirmed the move. He turned the volume up. "ZULU TWO-FOUR-THREE ON ONE-FOUR LEFT, BARKSIDE."

The Hughes APG-65 digital multi-mode radar burned into the right DDI. Les could see it was a large target. The readouts showed the aircraft to be ahead at a range of seven miles. He peered through the glass and the HUD, into the night, towards the direction of the dark, puffy clouds. No visual. Not yet. Two hundred knots was pretty damn slow. It had to be landing somewhere. Maybe the nearby island of Saipan.

"ZULU TWO-FOUR-THREE, THIS IS BARKSIDE. FIND OUT WHO HE IS AND WHAT HE'S DOING IN OUR AIRSPACE. WE ARE UNABLE TO MAKE RADIO CONTACT. OVER."

"ROGER, BARKSIDE. COMING UP ON HIS SIX. CLOSING AT 500 KNOTS."

Then the radar target disappeared off the pilot's radar. "BARKSIDE, THIS IS ZULU TWO-FOUR-THREE. IT'S GONE. REPEAT, GONE."

7

"WHAT DO YOU MEAN GONE?" LONG PAUSE. "HEY, YOU'RE RIGHT. SCOUT AROUND. FIND OUT WHERE HE WENT."

"ROGER, BARKSIDE."

After a thorough but unsuccessful search of the area, Les hit the radio transmitter. "BARKSIDE, ZULU TWO-FOUR-THREE. NO VISUAL. OVER."

"COME ON BACK, ZULU TWO-FOUR-THREE," the controller sighed. "NO JOY TODAY."

"ROGER, BARKSIDE. COMING HOME."

Les pulled hard right on the stick and increased the throttles until the speed flashed to *600 knots* on the HUD. The G-forces pressed against his body. . . 3-G. . . 4-G. . . This was the second time in a week that a large unidentified target had appeared suddenly on the Agana radar screens, only to vanish without a trace once a navy fighter approached it. Both times, Les was in the cockpit. He wasn't too concerned about it, though. Often, especially in the last few weeks, Andersen Air Force Base, situated on the north end of Guam, would send up their USAF bomber aircraft and the lines of communication with the navy would get crossed. Right now, that aircraft—whatever the hell it was—was probably about to or had already landed on Saipan.

On the way back, he set up his waypoints and followed them on the overlaid display on the MPCD. The south edge of Tinian flashed by, then the small island of Rota. The waypoint bearing readout showed 184 degrees. Before he reached Guam, he made the selections for the TACAN—the Tactical Air Navigation—a navigational approach aid that gave both distance and bearing to a base.

Coming in downwind at 280 knots, eighty percent RPM, speed-brakes out, flaps in the auto mode, Les had the nose up at nine degrees. He fell easily and controllably out of the sky with a twenty-eight-degree bank turn. He retracted the speedbrakes and leveled out. His airspeed dropped to 240. Two miles out, he selected *full gear down* and *full flaps.*

He watched the HUD closely. He lined up the velocity vector symbol on the horizon line. On final approach, he throttled back and lowered the velocity vector three degrees. Now he was coming in at 125 knots, 300 feet above the runway. Les loved landing the Hornet. Simple as pie, he often said. One big computer game. He lined the HUD velocity vector with the edge of the touchdown markers that were painted on the runway and brought the armed monster in for a perfect landing.

Lieutenant Les Shilling was a twenty-eight-year-old, fresh out of Fighter-town, USA, the famous Top Gun school in Miramir, California, where he completed a five-week training course with high honors. The calm, cool pilot had been a disciplined terror over the California desert. The instructors were impressed with the no-nonsense Shilling, who was rock steady at the controls. No one, including the instructors, had escaped him and his aircraft during the strenuous, competitive dog fighting. He could make the F-18 do what most other pilots couldn't. In short, he took to heart von Richthofen's words: "The quality of the crate matters little. Success depends on the men who sit in it."

Les relished flying, proud to be one of the chosen few. The US Navy stats spoke for themselves. Out of every thirty desirable applicants in the training program, ten went on to flight training. Four passed as pilots. Out of these four, only *one* was considered worthy to fly operationally. Les was that one. A notch above the rest. A naval aviator. An artist.

And he was part of a proud force—the United States Navy—who had never lost a war at sea. Going back to the War of 1812, the Americans, with a measly seventeen ships, held Britain's more than 600 vessels at bay. During the Second World War, the USN kept the sea lanes open to Britain and brought the Japanese to their knees in the Pacific, beginning with the Battle of Midway. Now, the USN was top dog in the Pacific, the only area of the world where they were not competing with the army and air force for recognition. Not so in places like Europe. Les had been stationed on Guam for five months now with a temporary special forces Hornet squadron, after coming over from Japan, where he had spent six months with another Hornet squadron. Prior to that he was attached to the USS *Midway*, home-ported in Yokosuka, Japan. Hornets in every case. His machine.

As far as Les was concerned, there was no other fighter quite like the F-18 Hornet, the aircraft to beat at Top Gun. This multi-role fighter scared many pilots at first. It seemed too complicated, too comput-erized, too damn expensive. However, it quickly functioned beyond original expectations. The power, the maneuverability, the lightness of the controls, impressed fliers. From the time Les first stepped into the

9

fighter, he found it unbelievably easy to fly, as if he had already been in it for months. He prized the visibility factor. He could see extremely well in all directions. He felt as though he was sitting *on* the aircraft. Not inside it. Damn good crate, she was.

Now in his work khaki, Les threw his gear in the locker marked by his callsign of HULK, and closed the door. Without a doubt a one-woman man, he was, a handsome, muscular specimen who often made the opposite sex's heads turn. He stood tall—just over six feet—and was richly tanned from the tropical sun. The strong, silent type, he was not one to waste words, almost taciturn at times, talking only when it seemed necessary. Only for something deemed important.

Turning around, he was suddenly and unexpectedly face to face with feisty Jack Runsted—callsign Tiger—another F-18 fighter pilot who had just finished an earlier night flight. Tiger was a skilled navy pilot who'd been bitten by the navy bug in his mid-teens. The women thought this six-foot bachelor was good looking enough, what with his blue eyes and short, curly, blond hair, although he was often irritating, arrogant, and a downright flake. Word was out that he was sowing his wild oats all over the island of Guam. While in a half-drunken state at a navy party a month earlier, he had even tried to make a pass at Les's wife. Les had calmly offered to re-arrange Tiger's face. Since then, Les avoided the young man with the Brooklyn accent. Today was no exception. Les turned to the hall, ready to leave. As far as he was concerned, Tiger wasn't there.

"The CO wants to see you in his office," Tiger said, breaking the silence. "Right away."

"Yeah. OK," Les grunted, over his shoulder.

A short stroll later to the CO's office, Les saluted his commanding officer, Captain George B. MacDonald. On the walls hung color photos of an F-14 Tomcat, an F-18 Hornet, and the same F-4 Phantom that MacDonald had flown in the Vietnam War.

"At ease, Hulk," the CO barked in his deep voice, looking up from his desk.

"Thank you, sir."

MacDonald's tanned face was long, with sunken, alert brown eyes. Nearing fifty, he kept himself in great shape, appearing to be a good ten years younger. A go-getter, he always wanted everything done in a hurry. And with precision. "What happened out there?" He leaned back in his chair, waiting. No expression.

Les took a breath. "Well, sir, the target disappeared before I could identify it."

"Disappeared?"

"Yes, sir."

"That's the second time this week. And you were there the other time."

"Yes, sir. That's right."

"Did you circle the area this time?"

"Yes, sir. Nothing."

"What do you make of it, lieutenant?"

"I don't rightly know, sir. It could be the air force are playing games with us."

The captain folded his arms. It was no secret that Andersen Air Force Base to the northeast, the old converted World War Two B-29 base, had been busy throughout the Mariana Islands all July with aerial activity. "The air force have been deploying some exercises lately where radio silence is vital. But I wish we'd know in advance so that we don't waste taxpayers' money sending up a thirty million dollar aircraft for nothing. Do you think it could have been the B-29 that's being repaired for the Second World War reunion coming up on Tinian? The—what's that squadron?"

"The 509th Composite Group, sir," Les replied.

"Yeah, the atomic outfit."

"It might have been the B-29, sir. The target was large enough. And it appeared to be landing. Maybe at Saipan. It never got above a thousand feet."

"But why this late at night." The CO smiled for the first time. "I remember your file. Your father was based with the 509th, was he not?"

"Indeed he was, sir. Ground crew."

"Is he coming out for the reunion?"

"I'm hoping he is, sir. I don't know yet."

"I'd like to meet him, if he does make it."

"You would?" Les tried to restrain his surprise. "Yes, of course, I'll let him know."

The CO smiled again. "OK. In the meantime, I'll see if I can find out what's going on. I'll make some calls. Dismiss, lieutenant. Go get some sleep. Say hello to Gail for me." Remaining in his chair, he snapped off a stiff salute.

"Yes, sir, I will."

Inside of five minutes, Les jumped into his newly-leased, white Nissan 240SX, opened the sunroof, and drove through the front gate. The night was warm. He opened the glove box and fingered through his assortment of 1950s and 1960s rock-and-roll tapes. Fats Domino, Ricky Nelson, Buddy Holly. . . He chose *Dion's Greatest Hits*, one of his favorites, and snapped it into the tape deck. There wasn't a car on the road, not at two-thirty in the morning during the week. However, he still stuck to the island's strictly enforced thirty-five-mile-per-hour speed limit out of habit. When *The Wanderer* came on, he cranked the music up good and loud, tapping his fingers on the steering wheel. Home, his wife, the sack, ten minutes away.

Two

Robert Shilling turned his back to the sun, wiped his brow, and continued vacuuming the pool in his swim trunks. It was a typical southern Arizona summer day. Hot, dry, no clouds. Now, at mid-afternoon, the temperature hung at a blistering 103 degrees. Shilling was feeling the heat. He was getting too old for this. Since his retirement in 1985, he had been thinking seriously of selling his sprawling suburban bungalow and moving into an apartment on one of the hillsides overlooking Phoenix or Scottsdale.

On the other hand, he couldn't bear the thought of wasting away the last few years of his life in some concrete high-rise. Besides, a mechanic by trade, he loved to work with his hands. And there was always plenty to do around the house.

"*There* you are. Come out of the sun before you fry to a crisp."

Robert spun around to see his wife, Edna, standing with a tray of two tall, frosty pina coladas. She set the tray down on the patio table near her, under the shade of the umbrella.

"Have a drink. Cool off. What are yuh doing out here, anyway?"

Robert sighed, adjusting his dark sunglasses. "Ah, the pool's so dirty. I haven't been able to get at it for a week."

"Can it wait? Sit down."

"Sure." Robert hooked the top part of the pole under the diving board to keep the vacuum system circulating freely. "Be right there."

"You're getting a little red on your chest," Edna warned her husband as he walked over to the shade of the patio umbrella.

"It's no wonder," he admitted, glancing down at his chest thick with white bristle. "I've been out most of the day."

"Naughty boy."

"I didn't think it was that bad. I could use one of those drinks right now." He plunked himself down in one of the white plastic chairs and placed his sunglasses on the table.

So far, retirement had been good to the couple. They were healthy and tanned, and both had stuck to a daily exercise program to keep the pounds down. Part of that program was golfing. At seventy, Robert had a full head of white, crewcut hair. He still had the broad shoulders from his youth, but age was slowly etching its evil way into his dark skin. The wrinkles were deeper and his voice gruffer. He had often said that he would have preserved his lungs and voice box if he had quit smoking earlier, instead of only ten years ago. Edna had been a smoker also, until shortly after her husband quit. Her face too had the telltale lines, which she thought was rather unbecoming for the Miss Arizona 1944 she had been. Nevertheless, she was still pretty with vivid blue eyes and dimples when she smiled. The sixty-four-year-old was still quite attractive in the one-piece bathing suit she was wearing.

She pulled up a chair and joined her husband in the shade. Noticing his war album on the table, she turned to him. "Reminiscing?"

Robert consumed some of his drink. He enjoyed pina coladas on a hot day. "I guess I am. You know, I haven't looked at it in ages. I wonder if I'll recognize any of those guys at the reunion?" His eyes grew large. "And will they recognize me?"

The couple eyed each other.

During World War Two, Robert Shilling had been a master sergeant with the United States Army Air Force, a crew chief with the famous 509th Composite Group on Tinian Island, the organization responsible for the world's first atomic bombing missions. Following his post-war discharge, he returned to his hometown Phoenix, married Edna, and worked as a mechanic for a Ford dealership in the city, the job he had recently retired from.

Staring at the open book of snapshots, Robert recalled—in a flash—some of his hard-working war years on the tropical island of Tinian. There had been no glory scraping his fingers to the bone keeping his crew's B-29 in the air. *Keep the boys flying* was the rally cry, much to the same degree as *Remember Pearl Harbor*. That was hard to do considering all the mechanical problems that plagued the first B-29s. The hours had been long, the heat unbearable. Often he was so tired that he would fall asleep in his work clothes because he was too weak to even peel them off.

"There it is," Edna said, bracing herself.

"Huh?"

"The *Mary Jane*. You had it open to the *Mary Jane*."

Robert set the drink on the table. "Yeah, missing in action," he said slowly, as if in a trance.

"They never found the bomber or the crew, did they?" she asked softly, hoping for a response. The *Mary Jane* was usually a taboo subject in the Shilling household.

Robert answered with a jerk of his head. "No one knows what happened. It just disappeared somewhere between Tinian and Japan, a couple days before the Japanese surrender. Geez, they were a good bunch of guys."

"A couple of days *before* the surrender? So it went missing after the atomic missions. After all these years. I never knew that!"

He sighed. "You didn't?"

"No."

"Ah, it was just a routine mission." Robert took a big gulp of the drink. "There was still a few conventional bombing missions after the atomic ones."

"Was there?"

"Yeah. A lot of people don't know that. Anyway, can we drop the *Mary Jane*?"

"Sure." She got the intent. No more talk about the bomber. At least not for now.

Robert's mind fell back to the war. He remembered how the aircrew had treated him and his ground crew with the utmost respect. They were a team, regardless of rank. The loss of the *Mary Jane* aircrew had struck Robert hard, as if he alone—the crew chief—was to blame for their disappearance. Due to guilt, he, at first, refused to attend the 509th reunion. Forty-five years later he continued to ask himself the tormenting questions. Were there mechanical problems with the engines? Was the bomber shot down by a Japanese fighter. . . or worse. . . by some

15

trigger-happy US Navy gunner aboard some battleship? No one would ever know. Then. . . more recently. . . he asked himself what difference it really made now. Why sweat it over and over again? It was then that he decided to go to Tinian. He and his wife needed to get away, see some old friends from the 509th and their two sons—David and Les—on the other side of the Pacific.

"Looking forward to the reunion?"

"Yeah, I guess so. Now I am."

"Have you heard how many are going?"

Robert took a long time to answer. Folding his arms, he said in a flat voice, "Including wives, something like four or five hundred."

Edna looked surprised. "That many? I can't wait to see Les's kids. They must be so big now. Did you read David's letter?"

"I did. He seems to be doing quite well for himself. The Midas Touch. But he didn't have to send us the air fare to Kyoto."

Edna chuckled. "He's got a lot more money than we do."

"That's for hell sure." Robert paused for a moment. "Sounds as if he's dating a Nip."

"This is 1990, dear. The politically-correct term in Japanese. No more Nips. Not even Japs."

Robert grunted. "Oh, yeah. So I've been told."

"From the sound of your voice it seems you don't approve."

Robert stared her down. He couldn't bear the thought of a Japanese daughter-in-law. Young people David's age just didn't understand. They didn't live through the war years. "What do you think?" he said curtly.

He still found the war hard to forget. His mind drifted back to how badly the American POW's were treated by the Japs. The Americans had taken Japan to their knees. After the war, the Japs turned around and whipped everybody else by selling their products cheaper. This was especially true in the car market. *Buy American* was Robert's personal motto. Keep the jobs here. But he seemed to be the last of a dying breed.

Edna decided to change the subject. "By the way, why are they not waiting for a 50th anniversary, instead of a 45th?"

"I wondered that, too. Maybe because we'll all be too old in 1995."

"What's on the agenda?"

Robert adjusted his chair, and told Edna what he knew. The usual assortment of breakfasts, lunches, and other get-togethers. *Fifi*, the world's only flying B-29, would make an appearance by flying over the runways at Tinian. Major-General Phillip Cameron, the pilot who had dropped the first atomic bomb, at the controls. Next, a couple tours of Tinian, with a windup gala evening on the third and last day.

"I can't wait. Two weeks to go. It'll be fun."

"Sure," Robert replied.

"Too bad it has to be in August. I heard that's the hottest month in the Mariana Islands. Les says it gets pretty humid there at times."

Robert shrugged. "It has to be August. That was the month we dropped the bombs and ended the war. It wouldn't be right any other time. Anyway, I'd better get back to the pool."

GUAM

Les was so sound asleep that he didn't hear the bedside phone ring. His wife pulled her tired body across her husband's bare chest and grabbed the receiver, warm from the sun's rays streaming through the bottom of the curtain covering the bedroom window.

"Hello," she said, gruffly, almost in a whisper into the receiver, as she lay on her back.

"Gail. It's David. How yuh doing? Yuh OK?"

She brushed the hair from her eyes and got up on one elbow. "Hi, David." She glanced over at the digital clock on the nightstand. "Guess we slept in. Hell, it's ten o'clock."

"Can I talk to my little brother?"

"Sure. He was out late. Didn't get back from the base 'til two or so."

"Out on maneuvers, was he?"

"Yeah. I'll see if I can wake him."

Gail glanced at Les, who was out cold. "Hey, Les." She was talking louder now. "It's your brother."

Les opened his eyes to see Gail looking down at him, inches away, smiling, hugging him close. Her long brown hair hung down over her nightgown. She placed the receiver between them so they both could listen.

"Hi, David," Les said, clearing his throat.

"How goes it, little bother?"

"Ah, well. . . hanging in there. What's up?"

"I got a letter from mom and dad. They're going to the reunion after all.

17

They said they plan to come up to Kyoto for a few days, too. I wanted to know if you and the family wanted to drop by with them. How about it?"

"Yeah, I suppose so," Les said slowly, struggling for the words, eyes squinting. "If I can get the time off. I'll have to see, I'll let you know," he went on, stopping to kiss his wife on the cheek, while she purred in his ear. "By the way, I didn't think dad wanted to go. What changed his mind?"

"Hell if I know. And he even wants to visit Japan for the first time. You don't suppose the ol' guy has finally mellowed?"

"Maybe."

"Get back to me as soon as you can, OK."

"Sure. A day or so."

"Great. Got to go. See yuh, navy boy."

"You bet."

Gail hung up for him.

"Hi there, Hulk," Gail said, her hand moving in his hair.

Les smiled. "Are the kids up?"

"I don't hear them. Close the door," she demanded, smiling.

"Now?"

"What's the matter, you not up to it? Hulk can't take it in the morning anymore?"

As Les got up to shut the door, she quickly sat up on the bed and removed her nightgown.

KYOTO, JAPAN

David leaned backwards in his upholstered chair and laced his hands behind his neck. He was already on his third cup of strong coffee this morning, inside his plush Kyoto International Hotel office.

David had found pleasure in the good life. While Les had the Navy, David was already a millionaire at thirty-two. A wise investor and businessman, he owned two hotels, several middle class and well-to-do apartment buildings, and two fine-dining restaurants, all in Kyoto, one of the most breathtaking cities in Japan. He was the fortune hunter of the family, having left the States in his twenties to take a business administration course at Tokyo University. Despite his mother's good-natured pestering, he still remained unmarried, although he did practice a lot. He had had girlfriends. A few affairs. Now for the last two months, he

18

had been dating a pretty Japanese girl. Things were getting serious. And they both knew it.

David stepped over to the attached washroom and stood before the mirror. He combed his thinning hair which was mostly dark, with a thin splash of gray around the temples. Shorter and heavier than his navy brother, David was handsome in his own right. The elder Shilling brother took pride in his appearance. Nothing but designer clothing. Suit, tie, shirt today.

Finishing his coffee, he turned to the window and looked down at the beautiful and historical Imperial Park fifteen stories below, where the imperial family had made their residence for centuries prior to Tokyo becoming the capital of Japan. His eyes scanned what he could see of Kyoto, a city surrounded by low hills. Off in the distance, miles away, he saw shiny Lake Biwa. The city of over one million people below was renowned for its hundreds of Shinto shrines and Buddhist temples. A good number of old buildings—the previous century and older—were still standing because Kyoto was a unique major Japanese city. It was completely untouched by American bombing raids during World War Two. Kyoto was a tourist attraction, which pleased David. That meant money. One unofficial tag for Kyoto was the Convention City. Visitors who came here had to stay in a hotel and had to eat at restaurants. And he had that ground covered. Furthermore, any students who attended university needed to reside somewhere and what would be better than one of his apartments near the campus.

David also liked the land, the climate, and the people of Japan. Grinning, he thought of his father and how he still hated the Japanese. The silly bugger. David shook his head and turned to his desk.

Three

"More eggs? One more helping left."

Les sighed, glancing up at Gail. "Sure. I'll take the rest."

The central air unit was going full blast at a quarter to twelve in the morning in the comfortably furnished rented house. The young Shillings liked the spacious bungalow. More room than they needed. The kids—a six-year-old boy, Darrell, and an eight-year-old girl, Fran—were in the den, just off the kitchen, playing with their toys as their parents sat at the kitchen table. Saturday morning for Les and Gail was time for coffee, a bite to eat, and relaxing. What Gail appreciated most in these settings was conversation. She always found her husband more talkative after lovemaking, as if a tap had been turned on.

"So, your parents are coming."

Les's eyebrows went up. "It had to be a last minute thing for pop. He's even going to Japan. If that don't beat all. Mom probably had to get after him. But I still don't know how she did."

Gail sat and poured herself a second cup of coffee, then laced it with double cream. "I know he doesn't have fond memories of the war, but I guess he wanted to see his buddies."

"Yeah. You know something?"

"What?"

"I never knew that he had been with the 509th Composite until I was fifteen. Even then, mom was the one that told me and David. He hated the war. And he still hates the Japanese. I don't know how visiting Japan is going to pan out." Les sighed, and shook his head. "There

21

was no glory in war for him. A lot of hard work. He wasn't too crazy about war movies either. One time David and I were watching *Tora, Tora, Tora* with him. He was fine until he got to the Pearl Harbor attack scene. Then he got up and left. Went to cut the grass. He never said a word for at least a day after that. Geez, tough guy to figure."

"Yeah," she replied. "But he's always good to me."

He sighed. "That's for damn sure."

Gail was also from Phoenix, Arizona. She could have had her own career had she wanted. But she preferred to be a stay-at-home mom and the wife of US Navy fighter pilot Lieutenant Les Shilling, the man she met on a blind date. She had taken nurses' training in Phoenix and completed the course.

Once marriage and kids came along, she chose to take only part-time work in her field. On Guam she was filling in two mornings a week at the navy hospital, while her kids were in school. She enjoyed the service life and was happy that her husband was now land-based and not out to sea on a carrier some place where she wouldn't see him for months on end.

The Shillings took advantage of what the tropical island had to offer. Along with the kids, they enjoyed swimming off the sandy beaches and windsurfing on the breezy warm waters. Les especially relished deep-sea fishing. Gail and Les usually kept to themselves, not making a habit of visiting a lot with the other couples. They still had close friends with whom they would double-date on occasion, but those times were kept to a minimum. Gail found some of the navy wives far too catty. In turn, some of the wives thought her a snob and her husband full of himself after coming back from Top Gun in May.

Piss on them, Les had said recently. He and Gail knew who their friends were.

ALBANY, NEW YORK

"Class," the attractive young teacher stood to address her Grade Eleven summer school history class. "As you know, we've been studying the Second World War. Today and tomorrow, we will concentrate on the atomic bombing missions on Hiroshima and Nagasaki. To gain a further insight into these events, we have with us today a resident of our city of Albany. The man who flew the world's first atomic mission.

Class, I would like to introduce retired United States Air Force pilot, Major-General Phillip K. Cameron."

The teacher—Miss Hay—looked to the open door. Into the warm room walked a good-looking man in his early seventies. His shoes sounded heavy on the floor. He stopped in front of the teacher's desk and eyed the classroom. He smiled and tipped his thick, horn-rimmed glasses at his grandson—who had made the necessary arrangements for his grandfather's appearance today—near the back of the room.

Born and raised in New York State, Cameron was an international personality of note. Since piloting the bomber that dropped the first atomic weapon in history, Cameron continued in the service until his retirement in 1964, when he went into his own mail-order business, selling military memorabilia. Retired fully now, he was appreciating the time with his wife. Money was no problem. He was in hot demand for after-dinner speaking and TV and radio appearances, and would even fly the occasional vintage World War aircraft at an air show. Patriotic to the core so many years after the atomic mission, Cameron still maintained he had done the right thing in dropping the bomb, despite the left-wing, anti-nuclear element of society that had been gaining more and more converts since the war's end. Besides, he was following orders. It brought a quick end to the war. No invasion. The bomb saved lives in the long run.

Today, Cameron had on a medium-gray business suit, with a light-gray tie. He stood straight and tall at six feet. When he dove into his brief introduction about his involvement in the atomic mission, he spoke fluently and coherently as if the mission occurred only yesterday and not 1945. After five minutes he stopped for some questions.

"General Cameron?" A chubby student in the first row held up her hand.

Smiling, Cameron looked down at her. "Yes?"

The girl stood. "Is it true that some members of your crew went crazy after the war?" Then she sat down.

"No, it's not true," Cameron replied, holding back a laugh. "That's a popular misconception about us. Many years ago the left-wing press took a certain piece of information and blew it all out of proportion. It all started when one of the crewmembers who had bombed Nagasaki happened to have some emotional problems prior to joining the air force. As the commanding officer of the 509th, I knew about his problems. At the time, he was not considered a risk. However, after the war he found himself in constant trouble with the law—drunk driving and what have you—and he was in and out of jail. He even wrote out an apology to the Japanese government for his crew dropping the atomic bomb on Nagasaki." He paused. "Getting back to the original question, I can assure you that all the living members of my crew are still in their right minds, and I hope to see them at a 509th reunion in two weeks."

Another girl from the front asked how much the atomic bomb project cost.

"Two billion is what I've heard estimated," Cameron saw eyebrows go up, "which is small in comparison to what the US government were spending in a month to finance the entire war against Japan and Germany, which was seven billion."

More eyebrows went up.

"General Cameron?" A boy from the back stood.

"Yes."

"What were some of the dangers involved in your atomic flight to Hiroshima and were you scared?"

"Yes, indeed," the retired air force vet replied, choosing to answer the second question first. "I *was* scared. But more scared that the mission would fail than I was scared for my life. First off, we were facing the danger of just getting the bomber off the ground with such a large bomb aboard. I had to use up every bit of the eight-thousand-foot-plus runway to take to the air. Then there was the concern of arming the bomb in mid-flight. Once armed, it was live and anything could happen." Cameron noticed the class was listening to his every word. "Then the biggest danger of all was what would happen once we dropped the bomb. Would the shock waves destroy our aircraft? Luckily, they didn't. But we still felt the wave when it hit us seven miles away from ground zero."

The teacher had a question. "General Cameron, would you mind telling the class how important you felt the bomb was? Did it have to be used?"

"That's a good question, Miss Hay." Cameron turned to her. "And I was expecting that question from someone today." He paused to gather his thoughts, then faced the class again. "In the early part of 1945, the

United States were drawing up plans for the invasion of Japan. It was code-named Olympic. Eight hundred thousand troops were to land on the southern part of Kyushu in early November 1945. By April 1946, a second amphibious landing, called Coronet, would be deployed on the island of Honshu, near Tokyo. As a result of these two pending invasion forces, the planners were expecting American casualties to number anywhere between a half million to a million men, and the Japanese casualties to reach well over a million. Up to that time, over 300,000 Americans on all the war fronts gave their lives for their country. The Japanese were a fanatical nation. We had no choice but to crush them. To this day, I still believe we did the right thing in dropping the bombs. We ended the war in a hurry, saved lives on both sides in the long run, and brought our boys home."

For several seconds, a period of silence engulfed the room, until a long-haired boy spoke from the middle of the room. "General Cameron, why were the cities of Hiroshima and Nagasaki chosen as targets, and not, say, a larger city like Kyoto?"

Cameron didn't hesitate. "Nagasaki and Hiroshima were considered military targets because of their war factories. Hiroshima, in particular, had many waterways and was easily spotted from the air, which made it ideal for picking out aiming points on which to drop our bomb. Kyoto, although much bigger than the other two cities, was eventually rejected because of the city's many shrines and temples that were revered by the Japanese. It was and still is a very historical city. And a very beautiful city too, I might add. For centuries it was Japan's capital. It was of very little, if any, military importance. Today, the Allied nations, Britain and the United States in particular, still face heavy criticism from bleeding hearts for the 1945 bombing of the beautiful city of Dresden, Germany, which supposedly had no military prominence. I guess the powers-that-be didn't wish to face the music again had they hit Kyoto." Cameron smiled, thinking how close Kyoto had actually come to being on the receiving end of an atomic bomb.

"Sir," asked another girl, "were there any more bombs in the atomic arsenal? What if the Japanese had refused to surrender after Nagasaki? Then what?"

Cameron smiled broadly. "Of course, we didn't let the Japanese government know, but we wouldn't have had another bomb ready for many more months. It was a good thing for us and them that they surrendered a few days following Nagasaki, otherwise we might have had to invade after all in the fall or wait till the atomic scientists had the next bomb ready."

The same girl then asked, "What do you say, sir, to the people who think we should apologize to the Japanese for dropping the bomb on them?"

Cameron wasn't smiling now. He waited several seconds before he answered. "I don't remember the Japanese ever apologizing for Pearl Harbor."

Four

Captain George MacDonald studied a large map of the Mariana Islands that his adjutant had placed many days before on the wall to the left of his desk. For the past week, the captain had been poking colored pins into certain spots on the map, an area north of Guam. Today, he punched two more pins into the paper.

The intercom buzzed.

"Yes," the CO answered quickly.

"Sir, it's Commodore Prentice. The connection isn't the greatest."

"Put him on."

"Aye, aye, sir. Line two."

MacDonald lifted his desk receiver. A moment later, a voice crackled, "George, can you hear me?"

"I can, Will. Bad reception."

"Tell me about it." Commodore William Prentice was the commanding officer of the carrier USS *Midway*, at that moment on naval exercises approximately 400 miles to the north of Guam. Although Prentice had recently risen one step in rank above MacDonald, the two were friends and had been since their early navy days in the States. "What's up, George?"

"Just thought I'd let you know that the two F-18 pilots will be coming up to see you in the next couple of hours."

"Affirmative. I'm too busy to worry about what appears to be some innocent target, anyway. I'm like Pontius Pilate. I wash my hands of the incident."

MacDonald grunted. He had a feeling they weren't so innocent. "Thanks for tracking down and recording the signals for me."

"I owe you one. Besides, we're in this together. At least as far as I can go with it. I'll make your boys feel right at home. Who are they, by the way? Anyone I know?"

"Lieutenants Runsted and Shilling."

"Shilling, huh? The Top Gun graduate." Prentice sounded impressed. "I'll be glad to take him back. I'll give them both the best treatment. And together we'll get to the bottom of this. Keep in touch."

"You bet. Thanks, Will. Let's keep this to ourselves."

"My lips are sealed."

"Good hunting."

MacDonald hung onto the receiver for a long time after the conversation, then finally laid it in place. Good ol' Will had come through. Thanks to him, *Midway*'s radar had been tracking the same targets once they were outside Agana's scan of 200 miles. MacDonald wondered what he would have done had *Midway* not been on naval exercises in the area. And what if he hadn't known Prentice? MacDonald felt a driving need to find the source of these strange signals that were now moving away from his base and were still suddenly disappearing without a trace before the navy fighters could get an ID or a visual.

A knock at the door made the captain look up. "Come in."

Jack Runsted and Les Shilling walked up, draped in their flying gear. Both gave the CO a firm salute.

"At ease. Come on over to the map, gentlemen. I want you to see something."

At the wall map, the pilots to either side of him, the CO stroked his chin and studied the map once again. Then he shut the venetian blinds to his right, to keep the setting sun out.

"On the map are six pins," he began, "placed on the exact positions that the mysterious targets were first recorded on radar. As you can see, there is a definite pattern unfolding. Two close together, a space, two not as close, a space, and two even further apart. They all form a perfect line." The CO's finger slid across the positions. "The northern point is almost 400 miles from Guam. The very first sighting occurred at oh-one-hundred July twenty-fifth, the second at oh-one-ten three days later, and the third at oh-one-fifteen two days after that. And so on. Six sightings at five or ten-minute intervals, but either two or three days apart."

MacDonald leaned against his desk and rubbed his neck. "Six sightings," he continued, "and we haven't made a visual. We have the hottest, most sophisticated fighters anywhere in the world with the most advanced avionics, and we can't even make a visual of an aircraft that's flying at a thousand or so feet and 200 knots!"

"Sir?" Les asked. "What about the possibility of flying saucers?"

MacDonald folded his arms and looked into the eyes of the two lieutenants. "It's something we'll have to keep in mind. Anyway, off the island of Agrihan is the carrier USS *Midway*. I want you two to take off at–" he checked his watch "–twenty-two hundred hours, and go straight for *Midway* and stay there until further notice. I want you both on alert, ready to be launched on a moment's notice. You each have a photo-recon pod aboard. Of course, you know what that means. I want pictures. No other action taken. The lab on *Midway* will do the developing for you. Then I want you right back here. This is just between us three. I want a lid on this. Got it?"

"Aye, aye, sir," the two pilots replied automatically.

"This is starting to piss me off!" MacDonald said. "I want to know what's out there. Dismissed."

Once the pilots left, MacDonald slumped into his chair. He was trying to sort out the events in his mind. The USAF claimed they were not sending up any of their aircraft in the early morning hours when the sightings occurred. In addition, *Fifi*, the B-29, had not been flying for three days, and the way things were going it might not even be ready for its Tinian reunion flight, now only five days away. According to the pattern, the next sighting was due at approximately oh-two-hundred tomorrow or the next day and should be off the island of Agrihan. MacDonald shook his head.

The whole thing was just too nutty. What the hell was out there?

USS MIDWAY

On the moonlit deck, Les and the plane captain checked the F-18 Hornet over. No leaks, no wrenches left in the intakes, none of the little things that could kill a pilot. No cracks on the tires or wings. The two satisfied, Les confidently climbed the ladder and slid into the cockpit.

He ran through the checklist, a handwritten set of notes on a piece of cardboard that he kept on his knees. He pressed the correct buttons for the navigation system, the radio, and on down the line. . . Then the deck crew gave him the all-clear. He fired up the engines, left to right. With the engines at idle, he waited for the crew to clear the parking chains and chocks. A young sailor in yellow—A Yellow Shirt—directed him by flashlight to the launch spot on Number One catapult. The Blue Shirts, complete with blue wands, scanned the F-18s control surfaces.

On the catapult, the hook-up man attached the launching bar on the nose gear into the shuttle. Then a Green Shirt took over and checked the holdback bar and its attached bolt, which would let loose only once the F-18 left the deck.

The on-deck speakers aboard USS *Midway* blared to life. "LAUNCH ZULU TWO-FOUR-THREE AND ZULU TWO-FOUR-FOUR! LAUNCH ZULU TWO-FOUR-THREE AND ZULU TWO-FOUR-FOUR!"

Green flashlight in right hand and red flashlight in left hand, the catapult officer directed Les. The officer zig-zagged the green light side to side. Les advanced the throttles to full. The Hornet's power wrenched against the holdback. While he pressed on the rudder pedals, the Blue Shirts checked to see that the rudders operated properly left to right.

Les watched for the catapult officer to move the green flashlight down, the signal for the pilot to push the throttles beyond the military range and onto afterburner. The light went down. Les lit the afterburners. The Hornet wrenched even more against the holdback. The hook-up man performed a final check on the launching bar and bolt. It was his job to do the final crawl under the aircraft before launching. He had a very dangerous assignment. If the bar wasn't attached properly, he could be run over by the aircraft. If he so much as moved the wrong way after crawling out, he could be sucked into the engine intake.

The scream of the full-throttled engines in his ears, Les saluted the catapult officer, then prepared himself. He glanced to his left at Runsted in his own F-18 on the other catapult. The mighty sound of four powerful engines could be heard for miles on the open sea. The two unarmed Hornets had been modified on Guam, each carrying an AAS-38 forward-looking infra-red pod on the port side, and a Martin-Marietta Laser Spot Tracker/Strike Camera on the starboard side, on the two positions otherwise occupied by Sparrow missiles.

Les looked up to his right, at the high, dimly lit superstructure. Inside was the Air Boss with his Flyco staff at the Flying Control Position. Below the superstructure, in the Goofer's Gallery walkway, where one could watch the deck proceedings in safety, were several deck crewmen dressed in their appropriate colored jackets. Only minutes before the yellow- and green-coated crewmen had been busy preparing Runsted and Les for the launch, once the Hornets had been brought up from below the elevators and spotted on the catapults. Now, these crewmen were squatting in the safety area between the two catapults. At the thumbs-up signal of the hook-up man, Les switched on his red and green navigation lights, which disclosed to all that he was ready.

The deck island lights turned green. Below deck, high-pressure steam built up in the steam receiver. The catapult fire button was pressed. The launch valves that regulated the thrust of the catapult with the exact amount of steam for Les's F-18 were opened.

The launch pushed Les's head back into his seat. The G-forces left him dizzy for a split second, until he was clear of the deck. He had just been propelled from zero to one hundred and thirty-five miles per hour in under two seconds. He remembered to keep his chin slightly down so that he could read the instruments and react in an emergency. Over the water, his wings grabbed the night air. He brought the nose up a few degrees, then the wheels and flaps up. RPM, fuel, oil pressure, hydraulics, registered normal. No surprise emergency lights on the right and left warning panels.

"BULLDOG, ZULU TWO-FOUR-THREE AIRBORNE."

"ROGER ZULU TWO-FOUR-THREE. SWITCH TO CHANNEL TEN."

"WILCO," Les replied.

The aircraft climbed rapidly. He leveled off at 2,000 feet.

"BULLDOG TO ZULU TWO-FOUR-THREE. TARGET ON HEADING THREE-FOUR-NINE. ANGELS THREE. ONE-NINETY KNOTS. RANGE—TWELVE MILES."

"ROGER BULLDOG. ZULU TWO-FOUR-THREE OVER."

Launched a few seconds after Les, Runsted came up off Les's starboard wing, some 100 feet away. "ZULU TWO-FOUR-THREE, ZULU TWO-FOUR-FOUR READY FOR THE HUNT. ARE WE LOOKING FOR A UFO, HULK?"

"QUIET," Les barked. "SPREAD OUT TO 300 YARDS. CLIMB TO ANGELS THREE. WE'RE ALMOST ON THE TARGET."

"ROGER, ZULU TWO-FOUR-THREE."

Through scattered cloud, Les was soon closing in on four red-hot exhausts. He lightly punched the radio transmitter. "ZULU TWO-FOUR-THREE TO BULLDOG. COMING UP ON BOGIE'S SIX."

With the aid of a camera connected to the radar, the Hornet's FLIR recorded for Les a positive identification six miles from the bogie, even before a visual was made. By selecting a 12x12 degree field of view on the throttle, a clear picture at night burned onto the radar display, the unmistakable outline of a four-engine aircraft. He closed down the field of view to 3x3 degree, an image magnification of four times. He recognized the aircraft immediately. He had seen pictures of the same type in his father's World War II album. A Boeing B-29 Superfortress. It had to be *Fifi*.

But why out here, this far from Guam? This—the B-29—was the source of all the trouble?

"ZULU TWO-FOUR-FOUR TO ZULU TWO-FOUR-THREE. SEE WHAT I SEE? WHAT GOES ON HERE? THIS SOME KIND OF JOKE? OVER."

"I DON'T KNOW. LET'S GET CLOSER. EASE UP AT 500 YARDS."

"ROGER."

At 500 yards away, the pilots brought back the throttles to a slow 195 knots, Les off the B-29s tail at eight o'clock level, Runsted at four o'clock low.

But before they could make radio contact with the target, they saw tracers in the night.

"GEEZ, HULK, THE CRAZY GUYS ARE SHOOTING AT ME! LOOK AT THE TRACERS. DAMN, THEY GOT GUNS ABOARD!"

"BREAK! BREAK!" Les replied. "I'LL GO IN."

Runsted shoved the throttles forward and quickly broke down and away, his afterburners blazing red-orange in the night. In seconds, he was far out of range, only a speck. Les pushed on his throttles and shot the fighter past the bomber's port wing, missing by 100 feet, all the time keeping a heavy thumb on the column's photo button.

INSIDE THE B-29

"COMMANDER TO TAIL GUNNER. ANY MORE ACTION OUT THERE?" the pilot asked over the intercom.

"NO, SIR."

32

"DON'T BE SO TRIGGER-HAPPY."

"I DIDN'T GET A REAL GOOD LOOK AT THEM, COMMANDER. WHEN THEY CAME PAST I THOUGHT THEY WERE BAKA BOMBS AT FIRST. THEN THEY BURST AWAY AT ONE HELL OF A SPEED, LIKE THEIR ENGINES WERE ON FIRE."

The commander hit the intercom again. "COMMANDER TO CREW. GET A HOLD OF YOURSELVES. WE CAN'T FOUL UP ON THIS. STOP AND THINK. THERE'S NOTHING BUT OCEAN OUT HERE."

"BUT I KNOW WHAT I SAW, SIR," the tail gunner pleaded.

The co-pilot looked over. "I saw something, too," he said.

The commander frowned. "NAVIGATOR?"

"YES, SIR."

"DO YOU HAVE THAT NEW COURSE FOR IWO YET?"

"YOUR NEW COMPASS HEADING SHOULD BE THREE-FOUR-EIGHT, COMMANDER."

"STEERING THREE-FOUR-EIGHT." The pilot-commander glanced at his compass and confirmed by adjusting his course. "HOW FAR TO IWO?"

"FOUR HUNDRED AND SIX MILES, SIR. AT PRESENT GROUND SPEED WE SHOULD BE THERE IN APPROXIMATELY ONE HOUR AND FIFTY-EIGHT MINUTES."

"ROGER. COMMANDER OUT."

The commander glanced behind and to his right at the flight engineer. The commander shot his right hand in the air—a slight wave—and smiled. In forty minutes, the flight engineer's mechanical handiwork would be needed. The flight engineer merely nodded, then resumed his duties, facing aft at his instrument panel.

Bent over the Mercator map at his desk with calipers and pencil, the navigator finished plotting the B-29s position by performing a double-check of his figures. First, he took the true course, which was the direction of the bomber measured in degrees. They were heading nearly due north. He took into consideration the wind direction, from the right in this case, and he added the figure to the true course to obtain the true heading. Next, he took the recorded minimal magnetic variation of that area of the Pacific and added it in, thus giving him the magnetic heading. He knew the bomber's deviation—the error in the plane's compass due to such things as radio disturbances—was zero. As a result, he now had the compass heading. Throughout the mission, he would give the commander compass reading changes on which the commander would turn.

In the process of making more calculations, the navigator was careful to differentiate between the True Air Speed (TAS) and Ground Speed (GS). He read the TAS off the airspeed indicator. The GS he calculated by pinning down his location, then dividing by time. He determined that in the last thirty minutes the B-29 had flown exactly 102.5 nautical miles.

Satisfied, he inserted the information in his log.

Time: 0202 local

Position: 14 miles NW Asuncion

True Course: 341

Drift Correction: +7

True Heading: 348

Variation: +1

Magnetic Heading: 349

Deviation: -

Compass Heading: 349

Temperature: +21

Altitude: 3000 feet

TAS: 216 knots

GS: 205 knots

Distance to Iwo Jima: 406 miles

Time: 0158

ETA: 0402

USS Midway

Carrier landings were always tricky business. Les knew it. He had never liked night landings, although he did consider them a worthy challenge, like pricking an Arizona rattler's tail. What was to enjoy in landing on a dark, pitching flat-top, often in windy and rainy conditions? It was enough to make at least a few aviators pack in the navy for good. Tonight, however, a full moon would make it a notch easier. Moonlight helped to ascertain the horizon, that sometimes unidentifiable separation between sea and sky. Les remembered two pilots in the last few years who had quit because of treacherous recoveries. This would be his hundred and thirtieth landing. Or trap, as they called it. He was hoping for an OK mark from the LSO—the Landing Signals

Officer—who stood to the port side of the deck, directing the incoming pilots. The grade, whatever it would be, would be displayed next to his name on the ready room chart. OK was equal to an A-plus. He didn't want anything to do with the inferior marks of Fair (not that good but safe), No Grade (dangerous for the pilot, crew, and carrier), and Cut (lousy, unsafe, could have resulted or did result in a serious accident).

Les switched the Hornet to the ACLS, the Automatic Carrier Landing System, also known as Mode One. He was over nine miles from the ship. The onboard computer would now take over and bring the fighter in at a sink rate of 600 feet per minute on a "hands-off" approach.

"DEAD CENTER ON THE GLIDEPATH, ZULU TWO-FOUR-THREE. BRING HER IN," the approach controller said over the radio.

Les took over the controls at one mile and continued to bring the Hornet down, coming in at a four-degree glidescope. The visibility over the nose and the angle of attack in a Hornet was excellent. Every little bit helped in a carrier landing.

Midway's deck, only 600 feet away, was unlit except for a series of lights along the edges and down the center line. The strategy on carriers in general was to aim the fighter's arrester hook at the third wire. Too low and Hulk would bang into the stern. Too far left or right and he'd hit parked aircraft. Too high and he'd have to settle for a "bolter," or go-around. Landing on *Midway* was especially tough because she had only three wires, as opposed to the bigger flat-tops, which contained six. In case he was forced to try again, he was coming in at standard procedure for navy pilots—full military power and full flaps. Minutes before, Hulk had been ordered to dump several thousand pounds of fuel into the ocean to lighten the load and make for an easier touch down.

Les picked up the orange ball on the landing sight, to the deck's port side. The green optical lights on the Fresnel lenses were in line. He had the right altitude and his wings were level. The deck raced towards him. Then he felt a solid *thunk* and a quick jolt to the body.

The wire caught.

He made it. Number 130. The hook runner sprinted up to the fighter and with a hand motion let the deck operator know that the fighter was OK to pull backwards to disengage the tail hook. Les knew how rough the hook runner's job was. It was only one year earlier on the same carrier that Les had seen an F-18 break loose from the arresting wire upon landing. The wire had cut the legs off the hook runner. The pilot had been so shaken he quit the navy.

When he climbed down the retractable boarding ladder, Les saw the silhouette of Tiger's Hornet, several hundred feet out, halfway on the downwind path. He noted wind gusts across the deck. The green-coated ground crew quickly pulled Les's fighter away to one side. From behind the barricade below the superstructure, he turned to watch Runsted on final.

"You're too high, you dope," Les said to himself, as his eyes went from the landings lights to Runsted's fighter, coming in full power. "You're too high."

Then as Tiger neared the deck, he lit the afterburners and pulled the Hornet's nose up. Over the sea, he banked to port. Les shook his head. Try again, pal.

The two pilots met a short time later by Runsted's recovered Hornet, just as the deck crew circled it.

"I couldn't control her."

"Crosswind?" Les asked.

"Yeah." Runsted frowned as he rested his hand on the nose of the F-18. Then, something caught his attention. A hole in the metal. He stuck a finger through it. "Geez, will you look at that," he said, frustration in his voice.

"That's a bullet hole," Les responded.

"Yeah, fifty caliber."

The two checked the aircraft over for other holes. None. The crew hooked the fighter up and towed it away, as the pilots stood there.

"What are we going to tell the captain, Hulk?"

"Simple," Les replied quickly. "We'll just tell him. . . a B-29 shot at us."

"Sure. Hell, yeah. Why not?"

GUAM

Captain MacDonald arrived in his Agana, Guam office before sunup to examine the infrared photo-reconnaissance pictures. He swiftly closed the door behind him, then flicked on the deck lamp before he sat down. He carefully opened the sealed envelope and laid the eight-by-ten photos on his desk.

He grunted aloud.

So. . . *damn*. . . it was the B-29. Is this what he was woken for at four in the morning? However, his irritation vanished once he took a second look. This was really strange. The bomber's markings weren't *Fifi*'s.

What the hell?

Five

Robert and Edna Shilling checked into the busy lobby at the Fleming Hotel, in the village of San Jose. There they received their reunion paraphernalia consisting of name tags, brochures on the 509th Composite Group and information on the island as it was today. And, of course, a room key.

Looking around the lobby and recognizing a few people, even remembering some names, Robert suggested that they drop the bags in the room and come back down.

They just got inside the room when the phone rang. Robert sat on the bed and went for the receiver.

"Dad, it's Les."

Robert broke into a smile, glancing up at Edna. "Hi, son."

"Sorry I missed you at the airport. I hope Gail took care of you."

"She did. No problem. Don't you have the perfect timing."

"How's that?"

"We just got into our room. So I heard you were on some exercise out to sea."

Les chuckled. "Talk about timing, huh. So, when will I see yuh?"

"We'll be back on Guam in—let's see—four days. Saturday morning. Arriving at nine."

"Right. We'll save the talk for the weekend, OK?"

"OK, son."

"See you Saturday. Have a good time. Can you put mom on?"

"You bet."

39

* * * *

While his wife took a shower, Robert pinched his name tag to his shirt and went downstairs to the cocktail lounge. About thirty people were casually milling about. At the bar, he took the last seat, and ordered a scotch and soda. Feeling a tap on the shoulder, he turned around quickly.

"Bob?" The voice came from a short, well-dressed man, bald on top, a cleft chin, and supporting a large stomach. He had what appeared to be a scotch-on-the-rocks in his hand.

Robert recognized the man, although they hadn't seen each other in forty-five years. He checked the name tag to be certain. "Tom. Tom Bates." He shook the outstretched hand of the former *Mary Jane* armorer.

"Geez, Bob, you haven't changed that much. You haven't put on a pound. Then again, look at me." They both laughed. "What have you been doing since 1945?"

Robert took his drink from the bartender. "Thanks." Turning back to his friend, he said, "Oh, the normal stuff. Got married. Worked. Raised a family. I became a full-time grease monkey for a Ford dealer in Phoenix. Retired now. How about you?"

"I went into real estate in Los Angeles during the big boom of the sixties. Then I retired to a ranch near Fresno, where I live with my wife. Lots of room for the grandchildren. Ride my horses. Light the barbeque. Pick fruit."

Robert smiled. "The good life. How many grandchildren you got, Tom?"

"Ten. I had four kids. Two boys, two girls. How about you?"

"Two boys for me. One lives in Japan. He's still single. The other, the youngest, Les, has two kids. He's the military man of the family, an F-18 fighter pilot in the navy, stationed on Guam."

"A son in the navy? That's great!" Bates gulped from his scotch. He turned away from the bar to look the room over. "Hey, isn't that Phil Cameron?"

Two sets of eyes shot to the entrance where General Cameron stood with his French-born wife. Several couples surrounded the Camerons, greeting them. The room suddenly came to life.

"See you later, Bob," Bates said, and left.

Cameron and another man, whom Robert recognized as Cameron's co-pilot on the atomic mission, approached the bar and fit into a space beside Robert.

"Two beers," Cameron announced to the bartender.

"Yes, sir." The bartender handed over two bottles of beer with two tall, clear glasses.

"Still like beer I see, Phil," Robert said, grinning.

During the war Cameron was a unique commanding officer. In charge of the 509th—a group strength of 1,700 men—he had his own private army. A team. First names. No salutes. No ranks. Just do your job and respect the other person and his job. But any leaks or loose talk. . . you were banished to Alaska or worse for the remainder of the war.

Cameron didn't utter a reply until he read the name tag. "Bob Shilling. It's good to see yuh." They shook hands. "It's been a long time."

"It sure has."

"You remember my co-pilot, Dick Hall?"

"Actually, we never did meet. Hi." Robert extended his hand and the smiling man gripped it solidly. Hall was a husky individual, blonde-white hair, well-tanned.

"Bob was the crew chief of the *Mary Jane*."

"Oh. . . really." Hall's smile vanished.

Robert expected the reaction. No choice but to change the subject. "Yeah, she was my ship." To Cameron, he said, "So, will *Fifi* be ready for your run over North Field tomorrow?"

Cameron forced a grin. "If they get the repairs done to her, I will. She's still in a hangar on Guam. They're going to burn the midnight oil tonight to get her ready."

"What's the trouble?"

"Engine number three. No power. I'm flying back tonight to see how things are going."

"Good turnout," Robert observed, eyeing the room. "Heard there's going to be over five hundred attending."

Hall leaned forward. "And once the 509th gets going, this sleepy little island will never be the same. We're going to paint her red."

Early in the afternoon the next day, Robert remembered Hall's words as he and Edna were on one of the many tour buses heading out in a convoy to the old 509th headquarters at North Field. From what he could see from inside the vehicle, Tinian hadn't really changed all that much since World War II. The only significant difference was the drop

41

in population. During the war, the island had been busy with activity due to the thousands of permanent and temporary citizens. Now, the population stood at 850, according to the driver—a small, dark-skinned man—conducting the tour. He told those aboard that he was Chamorro, that is, of Micronesian, Filipino, and Spanish descent and that he had been born on the island just after the war.

The tour continued through jungle and over hills. The driver spoke briefly of the many watermelon farms and the possibility of the United States setting up a military base once again on the island. This would be a great boon to the slow tourist industry. In addition, he continued, the long, flat topography of the island was suited for lengthy runways. Not only that, but if the Americans came back, and if the tax dollars were spent wisely, the islanders would receive better medical treatment and the best of schooling for the children.

Edna smiled. She was enjoying herself, amused that the streets were named after Manhattan throughways. The driver explained that when Tinian was captured from the Japanese in the summer of 1944, one of the US Engineering Corps who had laid out the island was from New York City and he had a great idea. Because the island was shaped like Manhattan, he wanted to bring a little bit of home to the Pacific. Thus, Broadway and 42nd Street was the most important crossroad. Other streets were Park Avenue, Madison Avenue and the picturesque Riverside Drive that ran along the water's edge.

Stepping down from the bus, Robert had his arm around his wife. Together, they watched the other buses unload on one of the old dispersal sites near Runway Able. The crowd was casually dressed for the heat, wearing shorts and light tops. Many were hung over from the late-night celebrating.

The sun was warm in the partially-clouded sky, with a slight breeze coming off the ocean. It looked like rain clouds were massing. This was the Mariana Islands' rainy season. A few hundred feet away, the surf was pounding against the rocky shoreline.

"So, this is it. Your base."

"Yeah, this is it," Robert answered his wife. "There's the 509th compound behind us. A nice monument marks the spot. And there"—he pointed—"are the four runways, all over 8,000 feet long.

Over there"—he pointed beyond the runways—"are the hard stands, where we did most of the work on the B-29s. In the summer of 1945, Tinian Island was the largest operational airfield in the world. That way is straight north." He nodded this time. "You can see Saipan only three miles away. More B-29 airfields were there too. And more again on Guam."

Edna squeezed her husband's arm. "Now, aren't you glad you came?"

Robert didn't answer. Instead, he turned his attention to a large, shiny aircraft coming from the south. Others soon saw it too. Then the *sound*. . . as the aircraft drew closer. After all these years, Robert could still recognize the distinctive roar of the four radial engines. *Fifi* had made it. He hadn't seen a B-29 in flight since the summer of 1945. Suddenly, the war came back to him like it had never done before. The long hours laboring away over the largest and most intricate bomber of the war. The stress. The worry. The aching arms. Then, for the first time in years, it all came out. His eyes began to water and he wiped them with the back of his hand. He was proud of his individual war effort. Really proud. He smiled at Edna, shyly, as she too began to get choked up.

Fifi banked out to sea and came around for an upwind landing on Runway Baker. Flaps down, the speed dropped off. By the time she touched down, Robert and Edna weren't the only ones in tears.

Six

"Mom, dad, you look great!"

Les greeted his father with a handshake and his mother with a firm hug near the parking lot outside Guam's International Air Terminal. His mother looked happy, keeping her arms around her son for a lengthy time. It was a warm day, all three in shorts and T-shirts.

"Have you put on some weight?" she asked, finally pulling back.

"Muscle. All muscle," Les grinned. "You two have lost a few pounds, haven't yuh. Anyway, how was the reunion?"

Tired-eyed, Robert replied, "We had a ball."

"And he's got the bloodshot eyes to prove it," Edna laughed.

"And to think you didn't want to go, dad."

Robert shrugged. "I know, I know. Your mother told me the same thing."

At the car, Les opened his passenger door for his parents, and then threw the two suitcases into the trunk. "Buckle up," he said, closing the trunk. "The laws are strict here."

Robert stared at the Nissan, not moving a muscle.

"What's the matter, dad?"

"A Nissan! You bought a Jap car," Robert replied. "What did you do that for?"

Les knew that his father—a confirmed Ford man—was touchy about Americans buying foreign cars, especially Japanese-built ones. "I didn't buy it. I'm leasing it."

"Don't matter. It's still a Jap car."

45

Les tried to remain calm. "Come off it. The war's been over for nearly fifty years."

"Not for me he hasn't."

Les and his mother exchanged glances, then Les said, "Would you rather take a cab?"

Edna nudged her husband. "Oh, for the love of Mike, damn it, Robert, get in the car!"

The Saturday morning traffic was heavy on Marine Drive, the roadway that led into the capital city of Agana. Les drove past hotels, car rentals, shopping centers, and restaurants, until he reached the beach where the shoreline palm trees swayed to the light ocean breeze coming off Agana Bay. The sunroof was back for Les and his parents to enjoy the sunshine.

For the elder Shillings, the contrast between Tinian and Guam—only 100 miles apart—was startling. Sparsely populated Tinian was laid back. Guam, with its 120,000 residents, was a beehive of bustle and activity. Les had the facts on hand for his parents. Five airlines serviced the island. It had seven radio stations, three television stations, three newspapers, and twenty-nine banks. Agana contained more than a dozen hotels, most of which had been built in the last ten years, as well as air-conditioned malls and plenty of fast-food restaurants. Guam was a far cry from sleepy little Tinian

"How about golf? What yuh got there?" Robert asked from the back seat, still pouting after the Nissan incident.

"The best. Admiral Nimitz Golf Course. I'll drive you out this afternoon. First, I thought we'd head home, pick up Gail and the kids and go for a ride around the island. Then a barbeque after. How does prime rib sound?"

"I like that," Edna replied, looking over from the front passenger seat. Robert said nothing.

"Oh, by the way, dad," Les said, glancing in the rear-view mirror at his father, "my CO wants to meet you."

"Really? What for?"

"I don't know. He just said he wants to meet you. You game?"

"Sure."

Later that afternoon, while the Shillings talked about old times on the

46

patio deck over drinks, steaks, potatoes, and Caesar salad, they were interrupted by the portable phone ringing on the table.

Les picked up the receiver. "Hello."

"Lieutenant Shilling?"

"Yes, it is."

"This is Captain MacDonald."

"Yes, sir, captain, what can I do for you?"

The conversation in the room died down, then stopped abruptly.

"Remember that meeting I talked about with you, regarding your father?"

"Yes, sir, I remember."

"I hear he's in town. I'd like to see him. Tonight. Eight o'clock sharp. I want you to be there too. My office."

Les caught a sting of authority in his CO's voice. What at first was supposed to be a so-called casual visit now sounded more like an order. He glanced at his digital watch. An hour to go. "Yes, sir. We'll be there."

"Keep this between the three of us, at least for now."

"Yes, sir."

The receiver went dead and Les hung it up. He turned to his family.

"What was that about?" Gail wanted to know.

"The boss," Les replied. "Relax, it's nothing. I have to leave in a while. I'll be right back, though."

The conversation started up again.

"Dad, let me top your drink."

"I can use some more ice, too," Robert added.

"Sure, come on in the house. I want to show you something."

By the time Les and his father arrived at MacDonald's office, two other people were already there. Tiger and General Phil Cameron. And what surprised Les the most was that Cameron and his father were on a first-name basis. Introductions were made. All five sat.

MacDonald yanked opened a desk drawer and pulled out a large manila file that contained photos and typed paperwork.

"Gentlemen," MacDonald began, firmly, "this is not a social gathering. It's business. Three weeks ago, Agana Naval Air Station picked up an unidentified target on radar at oh-one-hundred in the vicinity of Tinian. One of our own F-18s, flown by Lieutenant Shilling, was alerted. Before

47

he could make any type of visual, the target simply vanished without a trace." The CO turned to some papers in the file. "According to our radar, it was on a true course of three-five-zero degrees, at an altitude of 1,000 feet and a speed of only 200 knots. Another target appeared three days later at oh-one-ten over Saipan. It also disappeared without a trace. After a few more targets, I started to detect a pattern. They were appearing on radar every two or three days, and five or ten minutes later than the previous one, and at a speed of 200 knots. In addition to that, the position of these targets formed into a definite path north, as you can see, gentlemen, from the map to my left. I have plotted each radar sighting. Then a slight change occurred near the island of Agrihan. The target suddenly climbed to 3,000 feet and changed its course to three-four-one."

Cameron broke in. "Captain MacDonald, what in hell's bells does this have to do with Bob and me? The US Navy is none of our business."

"You'll see, general. Please let me finish. Shortly after oh-two-hundred hours, eight days ago, off the coast of Agrihan, Lieutenants Shilling and Runsted intercepted the source of these signals. And here's what they photographed."

The CO slowly spread out on his desktop six clear infrared black-and-white photos of a B-29 Superfortress. The others leaned forward to look. Les, Robert, and Cameron were all astonished. The pictures had been taken from the port side. On the tailplane was a large R inside a black circle, with the numbers 296546 below it. The nose contained the block letters **MARY JANE** and a life-like painting of a girl in a bathing suit below the pilot's window.

"I suspect," MacDonald continued, "that someone is playing a little game with the US Navy. This reunion of yours has attracted a lot of public attention. I've seen *Fifi*, myself, up close. This bomber, gentlemen, does not have the same markings, does it? In fact, the markings on this bomber are those of the 509th Composite. Your group, general. That's why I asked you and Mr. Shilling here." He turned his attention to Robert. "I did some checking, sir, with old Army Air Force records and found that you were the crew chief on the original *Mary Jane*. Do you two have any idea what's going on here?"

"No, we don't," the general admitted.

"I thought that *Fifi* was the only flying B-29 in the world."

"It is, captain. At least, we thought it was."

"Then why this? The *Mary Jane*? Obviously, there's two B-29s now." The captain frowned. "So, tell me, what's so significant about the *Mary Jane*?"

Robert and Cameron exchanged stares.

"All right," Cameron said to his old friend. "I'll tell them."

The general got up from the seat and paced the room, then stopped. "OK," he sighed. "The truth. Following the Hiroshima and Nagasaki missions, our government still weren't certain that the Japanese would surrender. Therefore, conventional missions were still deployed. On August 14, a bomber force was sent out to destroy the Hikari Naval Arsenal. The *Mary Jane* and a dozen or so others from the 509th Composite joined a group from Tinian's West Field." Cameron sighed. "The *Mary Jane* and, I believe, one other bomber, were shot down before they reached the enemy's coast. Both were never seen again. The next day, the Japs surrendered and all was forgotten about the *Mary Jane*. That is. . . until now." Cameron's finger pressed one of the pictures. "For some reason, somebody has made an exact duplicate of the machine."

"Why would anybody do such a thing?" MacDonald asked.

"You got me there."

"You sure this isn't *Fifi* disguised?"

"Positive," Cameron replied.

Les stirred in his chair. "I'd like to know one thing, Dad," he said to his father, "the picture you have in your war album at home didn't have a bathing beauty on it like it does on the picture, did it?"

"True," Robert answered. "That's because she was painted on the night before the mission. That's why. And there's something else. *Fifi* has most of the original gun positions still intact. *Mary Jane* was a stripped down bomber, as were all the other 509th B-29s. The armor was taken out. It had no blister windows, as you can see in the photo-recon shots. The only guns she was carrying were in the butt. In short, *Fifi* and this version of the *Mary Jane* are two completely different bombers."

"Now, the positions of these targets," Cameron said as he turned to the map on the wall. "I can see from these pinpoints, captain, that the course is working straight from Tinian towards Iwo Jima, the same approximate course that we used on our B-29 missions to Japan. Then, there's the times. May I see your paperwork, captain?"

MacDonald handed him the file. "Certainly."

"Thank you." Cameron removed the reading glasses from his breast pocket. He paused to read. "From this sheet, where the times, dates, and positions were plotted, I would have to say that the *Mary Jane* was right on time with her flight as it was proposed in the briefing. Your first radar sighting of her occurred at oh-one-hundred near Tinian. That was the time she was scheduled to take off. At oh-one-ten you sighted her on radar over Saipan. That figures. Then again you caught her west of Agrihan at oh-two-hundred. And her last marked position was 200 miles south of Iwo Jima. Your radar recorded the altitude at 1,000 feet until Alamagen. Then she climbed to 3,000 feet. After Agrihan she climbed to 5,000 feet." He sighed, eyes on the file. "Last sighting was 400 north of Guam. I see."

"General Cameron?"

"Yes, captain."

"Let me get this straight. You're telling us that whoever's in control of this exact replica of the *Mary Jane* is flying the exact flight path used during an actual World War Two B-29 bombing mission."

"Yes, that's what I'm telling you."

"And you don't know anything? How or why this is happening?"

"I do not. This is no publicity stunt on our part, I can assure you of that. We had enough trouble getting *Fifi* airworthy and off the ground."

"Stunt or no stunt," Les interrupted, "the tail gunner took a shot at Tiger's fighter and he's got the bullet hole to prove it. Fifty caliber."

"Is that so?"

"That's right, general," Tiger said.

"I'd keep an eye on this thing," Cameron said to the CO.

"We plan to."

"Good. These guys could be some wacky joy riders, or something."

MacDonald took the file from Cameron and said, "I have USS *Midway* available to me. I know the CO from the States. His ship has been training new F-18 pilots on carrier landings and he's going to be out in the area for a while. Tiger and Hulk, here, used the carrier as their base to take these pictures. It's not over. They will be on alert. We won't involve anyone else, at least for the time being. In the meantime, general, I would appreciate if you and your friend, Mr. Shilling, would stick around for a while and not leave town."

50

Cameron and Robert glanced at each other.

Cameron shrugged.

"Sure," Robert said. "We're retired. Nothing else to do."

Outside the captain's office, Robert cornered Cameron.

"That was clever, Phil. I hope the captain doesn't check into the *Mary Jane*'s real mission. That was quick thinking on your part."

"Was it? I hope I was convincing enough."

"You were." Robert put his hands on his hips. "What's your take on all this?"

The general folded his arms. "I think someone is playing a cruel joke on the 509th. I know I've made a few enemies over the years."

"Who'd want to embarrass us? And who the hell would take the trouble of reconditioning a B-29 to do it?"

"I wish I knew, Bob. Nothing makes sense, does it?"

"No, it doesn't."

They looked to Les down the hall on a wall telephone. They could hear him talking to his wife.

"So, your son's going to put us up for awhile, is he? That's pretty decent of him. But does he have the room?"

"No problem," Robert confirmed. "Look, let's go have a stiff one somewhere and sort this thing out."

"I'm with you." Cameron smirked. "It might take a few of them."

"Yeah, for me, too."

Seven

The mid-afternoon waters of Lake Biwa were a sparkling calm. One foot on his forty-foot cabin cruiser, the other on the dock, David Shilling helped his smiling Japanese girlfriend aboard.

"Toshika, I'm glad you made it."

"Thanks for asking me."

He kissed her lightly on the lips. "Yuh hungry?"

"I'm *starved*. Nice day, isn't it?"

"You bet."

David escorted her to the ship's stern. On a built-in shelf were small trays of food that held rice, pickles, fish, eggs, cheese, and sliced meat. The two sat at a table and ate, enjoying the warm sunshine. This past week had been a little warmer than usual, and the forecast for today was temps in the low eighties. That in mind, both were dressed lightly in shorts, T-shirts and running shoes.

Toshika was a slim, pretty woman in her middle twenties who spoke English fluently. A local history teacher, she was good-natured most of the time, sometimes bold and high-spirited, with a quick sense of humor. Her hair was midnight black, smooth, straight, and long, her unblemished skin a golden hue from the sun. David had met her two months ago when he was in the fashion shop she owned in downtown Kyoto, where he had been looking for a traditional Japanese dress for his mother. He had asked Toshika, who had broken off a previous engagement only that week, out for dinner that evening. They'd been seeing each other steadily ever since.

"My compliments to your chef, David. This is excellent."

They continued eating until a Japanese man dressed in a dark suit appeared from below deck. "Sir, is everything to your satisfaction?"

"Yes, it is. I'd like more tea."

"Certainly, sir." The waiter poured into David's cup.

Ten minutes later the table was cleared and the man, with the aid of another similarly-dressed man, cleaned up the food and trays and left the boat, leaving Toshika and David alone.

"Now, let's go."

"Yeah," replied Toshika, taking off her outer garments to show off her new bright-red, one-piece swimsuit. "What do you think?" She turned around for him.

She was stunning. David was impressed. "Not bad. Not bad at all."

In minutes, he started the boat's motor from inside the cabin and pulled away from the dock into the open water. Soon, he too stripped down to his swimwear, a pair of dark-green trunks. He kept the boat within a mile of the shoreline, moving slowly along, with Otsu City on his left. A few other boats were on the water.

"Check the fridge out," he said, nodding at the fridge in the corner, his hand on the wheel.

Toshika found a bottle of champagne inside. David urged her to open it, and she did. The loud "poof" startled her and the two laughed when some of the liquid sprayed the windshield and David.

"I didn't think opening champagne could be so much fun," she said.

"The glasses are in the cupboard, up above."

They clinked glasses and drank, standing side by side. Toshika finished her drink first and left to go topside to tan. After thirty minutes, David cut the motor a half-mile offshore and went up to see Toshika on deck, sleeping on her stomach. The closest boat was more than a mile away. He quietly dropped to his knees, picked up the suntan lotion beside her, and started to pour it on her bare spine between her swimsuit straps. She didn't wake until he rubbed the lotion into her skin.

"Hey," she murmured, coming to. She turned on her side, facing David. "We stopped."

"Yeah. Nothing to hit out here. I'll just let it drift. Thought I'd come topside and enjoy the scenery. You and the lake."

She chuckled. "Flattery will get you everywhere."

"I was hoping it would."

She glanced around at the water. "Nice, eh?"

"Yeah."

"Did you know Lake Biwa has special significance for many American airmen?"

"Really? What kind of significance?"

"For a short time during the war, B-29 bomber pilots used it as a rendezvous point for attacking nearby cities. They would stream in over the coast near Osaka, fly on and circle over the lake, then head for their particular target."

"I didn't know that." David was genuinely surprised and interested at the same time. "You learn something new every day."

"A person should never stop learning."

"Spoken like a true teacher. You're not like a lot of Japanese people. You find it easier to talk about the war."

"Maybe because my relatives were from Kyoto, one of the few cities unscathed by the B-29s. We were lucky that way. If I had come from Hiroshima or Nagasaki, I might not be so willing because the memories would be so close. Actually, when it comes right down to it, if my relatives had come from Hiroshima or Nagasaki, I probably wouldn't be alive today."

"Yeah, I guess you're right."

"Your father was in the war, wasn't he? Didn't you say he was a mechanic in the Mariana Islands?"

David hesitated. "Yeah, he was."

"Fighters? Bombers?"

He hesitated again. "Bombers."

"B-29s?"

"Good guess. Not only that, but he was part of the 509th Composite, the bomber group on Tinian that dropped the atomic bombs."

Toshika sat up. "Talk about learning something new every day. Why didn't you tell me this before?"

He shrugged. "You didn't ask."

"You were hiding it from me. Did you think I'd be angry with you?"

"I don't know."

"The war's been over for forty-five years. Neither of us were even involved. Besides, a man who used to fly B-29s—or he had some connection with them—is a very good friend of the family." She thought for a moment. "We always address him as colonel. He doesn't talk too much about the war."

"Neither does my father. But he still carries it around with him." He grunted and frowned. "What a guy. Geez, he doesn't like Japanese. Nor their cars. I hope that when he and my mother come to visit he'll change his mind once he meets you and my other friends."

"I see. So we're. . . well. . . goodwill ambassadors are we for Papa Shilling?"

"Not really. But it'll help. Another thing, if my mother sees me with you, she might think we're very serious about each other and she won't bug me about getting hitched. . . ah, married. Like she always does."

Toshika stood up, David with her.

"*Are* we serious, David?" She placed her arms around his neck. Before he could answer, she kissed him. "You're not trying to get me drunk, are you?" she asked, her eyes glassy.

"No."

"Are you going to take advantage of me?"

"Of course not. But you do look fantastic today."

"Thank you."

Hand in hand, they strolled to the topside rail, stopped, and looked over the water.

"David?" she said, her eyes to the water.

"Yes?"

"Do you want to know why I broke off the last relationship?"

He shrugged, gently. "If you want to tell me, I'll listen."

"All he wanted to do was go to bed with me. I couldn't do it. He was just too possessive. Not only that, but I made a vow to my father that I would stay pure until my wedding day. I'm a twenty-five-year-old virgin. In this day and age, you probably think that's funny."

David answered quickly. "Not at all. I think that's very honorable and proper."

"You do?" She turned to him.

"Yep. The man who marries you will be a lucky man. You must love your father very much to make such an important vow."

"I do love him. What about you? Do you love your father?"

David took a long time to answer the biting question. "He's a difficult

56

man. We haven't got along since I moved to Japan. I still don't know about this visit. I wish my mother would come alone. She's a lot more fun and. . . more accepting of others, regardless of, well, you know."

She nodded. "I know. Race, creed, religion, and whatever."

"Exactly." He took her in his arms. "Look, can we talk about something else?"

Eight

The B-29 commander knew that darkness would surround the bomber for another two hours. They were approaching the half-way point of their mission.

He swung his attention to the transmitter control box on the fuselage to his left. He turned the transpower switch to ON and set the frequency selector switch to the desired low-frequency band. Then he set the TONE-CW-VOICE switch to TONE. All was in order to transmit an important message to Iwo Jima. He pushed the throat mike to his Adam's apple with his left hand and with his right thumb pressed the PUSH-TO-TALK switch on the control wheel.

"Hawkeye three-six to Baker two. Fat baby getting spanked," he said in a slow voice. The commander didn't bother to wait for a reply. Due to previous orders, he knew that no one would answer. The receiving station's instructions were only to absorb the message.

The commander nodded at the flight engineer, who left his chair and went into the next compartment. The engineer winked at the radio operator on his left. He stopped by the edge of the hatchway that led to the bomb bay. There he was met by an individual in glasses and flight gear, coming through the tunnel above him. His nickname was "Four Eyes." The two opened the hatch towards them and crawled in. Now they were inside the dark and wind-whistling bomb bay, their backs to the open hatch. Attached to the top of the bomb rack was a long, six-ton, cylinder-shaped metal object. With the help of a strong flashlight, the man in glasses read silently from a piece of paper:

59

Checklist for loading charge in plane with special breech plug (after all 0-3 tests were complete)

1. Check that green plugs were installed.
2. Remove rear plate.
3. Remove armor plate.
4. Insert breech wrench in breech plug.
5. Unscrew breech plug, place on rubber pad.
6. Insert charge, 4 sections, red ends to breech.
7. Insert breech plug and tighten home.
8. Connect firing line.
9. Install armor plate.
10. Install rear plate.
11. Remove and secure catwalk and tools.

Four Eyes took some tools from the metal box left inside the bay and with the flight engineer as his assistant, went to work on the object. After a few minutes, the engineer stuck a hand through the hatch and held up three fingers for the radio operator to see, who in turn pressed his intercom.

"NUMBER THREE COMPLETE, COMMANDER."

"ROGER."

The commander's thumb went to the PUSH-TO-TALK switch.

"HAWKEYE THREE-SIX TO BAKER TWO. NUMBER THREE COMPLETE."

By the time Four Eyes reached the point of injecting the gunpowder and charge, he wiped his brow and took a deep breath to calm himself.

"Steady, boy," the flight engineer encouraged him as he handed the perspiring man the proper wrench.

Four Eyes followed step Number Six carefully. Finally, he inserted the gunpowder into the four sections, connected the firing line, and with exactly sixteen turns tightened the breech plate.

The flight engineer stuck a clenched fist through the hatch.

"NUMBER EIGHT DOWN, COMMANDER," the radio operator said.

"Here we go again," Les Shilling said to himself. Punching through the F-18's radio frequencies, he tried to contact the B-29, only 2,000 yards astern to the bomber at two o'clock high.

"ZULU TWO-FOUR-THREE TO TWO-NINE-SIX-FIVE-FOUR-SIX. DO YOU READ?"

Les had no choice but to try contacting the B-29 by using its six-digit original factory numbers as seen and documented from the photos. After some minutes, he heard what was probably the bomber trying to make contact on a low-frequency band with another party, which wasn't answering.

He would wait. . . and listen in.

Working quickly now, Four Eyes tightened the armor and rear plates.

"THAT'S IT, COMMANDER."

"HAWKEYE THREE-SIX TO BAKER TWO. FAT BABY WIRED FOR SOUND."

The flight engineer patted Four Eyes on the back. Wiping his brow with a handkerchief, Four Eyes looked relieved the job was over. All that was left—later—was to exchange the green plugs for red ones.

Les had something to go on now. "ZULU TWO-FOUR-THREE TO HAWK-EYE THREE-SIX. DO YOU READ?"

An answer came quickly. "ZULU TWO-FOUR-THREE. THIS IS HAWK-EYE THREE-SIX. WHO ARE YOU? OVER."

"I WAS GOING TO ASK YOU THE SAME QUESTION. WHAT ARE YOU DOING OUT HERE IN THAT OLD CRATE? OVER."

The commander glanced across at his pilot. "What's with this joker? What kind of callsign is Zulu with three numbers?"

"Zulu!" the pilot said.

"Yeah. Doesn't he know the Able-Baker alphabet?"

"Guess not. How dare he call our airplane a crate."

"Yeah. Yuh see anything?" the commander asked.

The two pilots strained into the night sky through the Plexiglas to either side.

Nothing.

"COMMANDER TO TAIL GUNNER. DO YOU SEE SOMEONE FOLLOWING US?"

"YES, SIR. THERE'S SOMETHING OUT THERE. A FIGHTER, I THINK. HE'S STAYING BACK AT 2,000 YARDS."

"NO ID?"

"NO, SIR. TOO FAR AND TOO DARK."

The commander took a breath and pressed the R/T. "CRATE, HUH? WHAT DO YOU WANT, LITTLE FRIEND? IF YOU ARE A FRIEND."

"I'VE CAUGHT UP TO YOU. NOW TURN AROUND AND LAND IT."

The two pilots exchanged bewildered glances.

"Caught up to us? What's with him?" the commander wanted to know.

The pilot shrugged. "Maybe it means an abort."

"An abort?"

"We're out of radio range. Maybe something's gone wrong. He does sound American."

"I REPEAT. TURN HER AROUND. IF YOU DON'T I'LL BE FORCED TO TAKE ACTION."

"ARE YOU AMERICAN?" the commander answered.

"AFFIRMATIVE. WHY?"

"HOW MANY HOME RUNS DID BABE RUTH HIT IN 1927?"

Les couldn't believe his ears. These guys were really playing the game to the hilt. Little Friend was an American World War Two term for a friendly fighter. Big Friend for a friendly bomber. And asking how many home runs Babe Ruth hit in 1927 meant that these guys were trying to find out if he was an American or not.

Les shrugged. Sure, he'd go along with them. "THE BABE HIT SIXTY THAT YEAR, BIG FRIEND."

"LET'S HAVE A LOOK AT YUH, LITTLE FRIEND. COME UP ON PORT."

"LAST TIME WE DID, YOUR TAIL GUNNER TOOK A SHOT AT MY WING-MAN."

"THAT WAS YOU, WAS IT? COME ON UP. WE WON'T BITE."

Shilling pushed the throttle forward and eased through the night sky. In seconds, the B-29 grew larger through the canopy. Twenty-five yards off and above the B-29's long port wing, he throttled back.

Inside the bomber cockpit, the commander and the pilot stared in astonishment at the F-18's needle nose and twin tails, silvered by the half-moonlight. For a long moment they couldn't speak.

"IS THIS CLOSE ENOUGH FOR YOU, HAWKEYE THREE-SIX?"

"WHAT THE BLAZES IS THAT?" the navigator yelled over the intercom.

"WHAT YOU GOT THERE, LITTLE FRIEND? WHAT KIND OF MACHINE IS THAT?"

"ARE YOU KIDDING ME? SHE'S A US NAVY F-18 HORNET."

"WHERE'D YUH GET IT?"

"WHAT! WHERE YUH BEEN, BIG FRIEND?"

"The Navy must be holding out on us," the pilot said to the commander, his eyes on the strange fighter off port.

"I SAY AGAIN, TURN BACK, HAWKEYE THREE-SIX," the fighter pilot's voice demanded.

"WHAT IF I SAY NO, ZULU TWO-FOUR-THREE?"

Les blew up. "DON'T GIVE ME THAT CRAP. GET THIS CRATE DOWN AT THE NEAREST ISLAND OR I'LL BLAST YOU TO KINGDOM COME WITH A HEAT SEEKER."

"I DON'T KNOW WHAT YOUR ORDERS ARE, LITTLE FRIEND. I'M LOSING PATIENCE WITH YOU. MY ORDERS ARE NO ABORT UNLESS I GET CONFIR-MATION. AND YOU BETTER NOT DO ANYTHING WITH YOUR—WHATEVER YOU CALL IT—BECAUSE THERE WON'T BE ANYTHING LEFT OF YOU OR ME, PAL, BELIEVE ME."

GUAM

Gail got up Saturday morning before the kids and the guests did. She put the coffee on and turned the radio to the local station giving the stateside major league baseball scores. She tied her housecoat a little tighter around her slim waist, then sat at the table to enjoy the quiet of the kitchen. Soon she was joined by Cameron's wife, Denise, a tall, graceful woman in her mid-sixties.

"The coffee smells good. The men will be sawing logs for a while," Denise said in her French accent. "I thought they had their fill at the reunion."

"Apparently not," Gail replied.

"I'll take a shower, Gail, if you don't mind."

"Go right ahead."

While Denise ran the water, the kitchen phone rang. Gail reached for it.

"Mrs. Shilling?"

"Yes."

"Captain MacDonald calling. Is General Cameron available? I need to speak to him."

"He's. . . still sleeping, I think."

"Would you wake him, please? It's important."

"Yes, sir, I will."

Gail set the receiver on the counter and made her way down the hallway to the guest room. She tapped lightly on the half-opened door that blocked her view of the bed. "General Cameron?" She knocked again. "General Cameron?"

She heard a groan and some bed sheets ruffling in the darkened room. "Yes?"

"Captain MacDonald from the naval base is on the phone. He said it's important. You can take the phonecall in there, if you like."

"Ah, yeah, thanks, Gail. I will."

Gail gently closed the door, went to the kitchen, and when she heard Cameron greet Les's CO, hung the kitchen receiver up.

Inside the guest room, Cameron sat on the edge of the bed, his eyes nearly closed, the phone held loosely against his ear. His head was slightly dizzy from rising too quickly. "Hello."

"OK, General Cameron. I'll get to the point. I made some phone calls to the air force archives in the States. I did a little checking about the *Mary Jane*. Apparently, she didn't disappear on the August 14 raid to Hikari, like you said. In fact, the *Mary Jane* didn't fly that mission. None of the 509th bombers went that day or any other day. They never flew any conventional bombing missions at all during the war. Another thing, do the callsigns Hawkeye Three-Six and Baker Two mean anything to you?"

Cameron's eyes suddenly opened. "Where did you get those call-signs?"

"How about 'Fat Baby wired for sound?' Does that ring a bell?"

"It might," Cameron admitted.

"It should. I've got another. 'Hawkeye Three Six to Baker Two. Number Eight complete.'"

"All right, captain, I get the picture."

"I wouldn't mind the whole truth this time, General Cameron. From A to Z. We need to meet somewhere. Breakfast is on me. There's a place on Marine Drive called the Round Top. I can reserve a private booth where we can talk."

The general sighed heavily into the receiver. "You may not want to hear what I know."

"Try me. . . sir."

The heat and humidity had already taken root in the early morning as Robert Shilling drove Les's station wagon down Marine Drive, he and Cameron deep in conversation.

"What do you think, Bob? Would you arrive at the same conclusion?" Cameron asked, his arm resting on the edge of the door. The front windows were down in the car, the two enjoying the breeze.

Robert grunted. "It's too hard to believe, but you have to admit that it explains a lot. The callsigns. The codes. But damn it, Phil, this isn't a science fiction movie. These things just don't happen. I still think someone is playing a trick on the 509th."

"I don't. This is real."

"What if MacDonald doesn't believe you?"

"What do you mean, *me*?"

"You outrank me, remember, and you were the commanding officer of the 509th. He might believe this if it comes from you. I'll put my two cents in when it's needed. Just state it in such a way that MacDonald will have to arrive at only one logical conclusion."

"Easier said than done, Bob."

The Round Top was crowded, with many of the customers in navy uniforms. Cameron gave his name at the counter, and he and Robert were quickly taken to a private booth—partially enclosed by a wall on three sides—where MacDonald, Les, and Jack Runsted were seated. As soon as they sat down, a chubby blonde waitress arrived.

"We'll all take the breakfast special," MacDonald said. "Could we have the coffee right away?"

"Yes, sir."

Once the waitress disappeared, MacDonald turned to Cameron and Robert. "All right you two. We're in this together. So let's have it. The true story about the *Mary Jane*. What happened to her? And what's with all those strange callsigns and radio talk that Hulk picked up this morning near Iwo Jima?"

Cameron removed his windbreaker and laid it on the chair behind him as the coffee came. The waitress poured and left. Cameron left his black and he stirred it. . . waiting. . . stalling. He looked over at his vet friend. "The truth. OK, here goes." He leaned forward. "Following the Hiroshima and Nagasaki missions, the United States still weren't certain whether the Japanese would surrender. We had no word from them. Therefore, in anticipation of them not surrendering, a third atomic mission was scheduled. The order came from the top. President Truman. The target would be the city of Kyoto, with a plutonium bomb that was more powerful than the first two atomic bombs put together. An estimated destructive force that could kill 200,000 people and injure another 300,000. History never knew about that mission. *Mary Jane* was the designated bomber deployed to carry out that third atomic mission on the morning of August 11, 1945. The crew was briefed the night before. They took off from Tinian at oh-one-hundred and," Cameron paused, "they were never seen again."

"Go on," MacDonald said.

"Did you notice that I said the *crew* was never seen again?"

"I did."

"Here's the dope. Even you, Bob, don't know this. The bomber was found on Guam the following morning."

"It was?" Robert answered, caught by surprise.

"Yes. One day after the Kyoto mission."

"Just the bomber?"

Cameron nodded. "Yes, Bob. The *Mary Jane* was discovered, intact, resting in the jungle near Agana Naval Air Station. The bomber didn't have a mark on it. I saw it. No signs of a crash landing. No bodies found on Guam or in the water. There was approximately five minutes of fuel left, if that, in the wing tanks. The fuselage contained four bullet holes. Under attack, I suppose. To add to it, a series of bloodstains led from the cockpit all the way to and inside the bomb bay. It was the craziest thing I had ever seen. It should have had crash damage to it. But didn't. The vegetation wasn't touched, except for underneath the wheels. It was as if she had plunked down neat as could be in the middle of the night, and someone found it next day."

"So, what happened to her after that?" MacDonald asked.

"We sensed something evil about the whole thing. Seeing that the mission was never completed, anyway, and the crew were never found, the bomber was supposed to be disposed of. At least, that's the story I got. Our scientists had no more atomic bombs. Three days later, the Japs surrendered. We were all sworn to secrecy. Captain, you wanted to know about the callsigns?"

"Yes."

"I hear Les had made contact with the *Mary Jane*. That true?"

"That's correct, sir," Les replied.

Cameron smiled slowly. "Les, did the pilot have a Georgian accent?"

"Yes, sir, he did. A very slow southern drawl."

"Captain Clayton," Cameron said to Robert. Then to MacDonald he said, "The callsigns are correct, captain. The ones used on the actual 1945 mission. Hawkeye Three-Six was designated for Clayton's bomber. Baker Two was Iwo Jima. When Clayton said that Number Eight was complete, he was notifying the scientists on Iwo Jima that Number Eight on the checklist of eleven points for arming the bomb was complete. The critical stage was done. An explosives expert from the US Army, an odd fellow we called Four Eyes because he wore a pair of thick glasses, was to accompany the flight and was to arm the bomb with the flight engineer's help." The general paused for a moment, reflecting on the crushed glasses he had found on the cockpit deck forty-five years ago. "'Fat Baby wired for sound' was the signal to tell the scientists that the bomb had received the first arming stage, with the final arming coming later in the flight, where Fat Baby would be fully live. Over Iwo Jima, they were to climb to 9,500 feet. Where was your interception made, Les?"

"South of Iwo Jima, sir."

"What altitude?"

"Five-thousand feet."

"So, they must have climbed by now."

"You're speaking as if they are. . . still on the mission."

"That's right, captain. I am. This might sound totally insane and after this you might have me committed, but I am convinced that you have intercepted the real *Mary Jane*. And she's carrying a lethal atomic bomb."

The men fell silent. "A real atomic bomb!"

"Yes, captain."

"This isn't the movies," the captain said. "This. . . this is 1990." He rubbed his face. "You're talking like some science fiction novelist."

"No. Not at all. But I am talking time travel."

"That explains it," Les exclaimed. "When the bomber refused to land, I told the pilot that I'd blast him from the sky. And he said that I better not do that because there wouldn't be anything left of the bomber or me."

"I don't believe it," MacDonald scoffed. "General, how could you arrive at such a hypothesis? You're no scientist."

"I didn't say I was. I'm looking at this as level-headed as I can, considering all sides."

"Time travel is only a theory."

"No so, captain." Cameron pulled out a paperback from the pocket of his windbreaker. "On the flight over from Los Angeles, I was reading an interesting book that I purchased at the LA Airport." He showed the cover to the navy captain.

"The Devil Seas. So?"

"The author," Cameron said, "has documented evidence of two areas of the world where strange disappearances have occurred over the last forty years or so. One of these areas is the Bermuda Triangle in the Atlantic. The other is in the Pacific, another triangle, directly opposite the Bermuda Triangle, should one drill a hole through the center of the earth."

The general showed the others the paperback's second page, a map of the portion of the Pacific that stretched from the Mariana Islands to Japan. A triangle was drawn over a large piece of the map. To the left of the middle of the triangle was Iwo Jima. Just outside the northerly point was Kyoto. Nudging the southern edge was Guam.

"Inside the triangle," Cameron went on, "hundreds of disappearances have taken place. Ships, subs, people, aircraft. Many of those military aircraft. All have vanished without a trace. The largest vessels were over 200,000 tons. Very few radio signals were recorded, signifying that they vanished too quickly to even reach a transmitter to voice an SOS."

MacDonald folded his arms. "How does this book prove time travel?"

Cameron held up two fingers. "Two stories. The first, October, 1962. Broad daylight. A DC-8 passenger jet en route from Tokyo to Guam. Just after take-off, several people aboard claimed to have seen a Japanese World War Two Betty Bomber pull up near the port wing, then bank away. One of the passengers was in the US Navy and knew his aircraft.

"The second, 1968, at the height of the Vietnam War. Many of us know that Andersen Air Force Base on the north end of Guam was used as a bomber base for the B-52s during the bombing campaign. This same field deployed Superfortresses during the Second World War. North Field, we called it then. Anyway, in 1968, also in daylight, a B-52 took off on a training run, turned north and flew 300 miles before turning south again. Twenty miles out of Guam, during the descent, the pilot and co-pilot both swore they saw a B-29 Superfortress flying in the opposite direction, a thousand feet below.

"What's so unusual about these sightings? Well, according to the author, neither aircraft—the Betty bomber or the B-29—existed in vintage form in those years. There may be a reconditioned Betty somewhere today, although I doubt it. But I know for a fact that there were absolutely no B-29s in flying condition in 1968. *Fifi* was not resurrected until the seventies, cannibalized from several other B-29s in the Mojave Desert. *This* Pacific triangle is a time barrier," Cameron concluded, tapping his finger on the map.

MacDonald smacked his lips. Still unconvinced, he asked. "Tell me something, general. Do you recall anything, any stories at all, about this Pacific Triangle while you were stationed here during the war? Crazy things must have happened then too."

"Hell! We had enough to worry about fighting the Japs."

MacDonald smiled. "Well–"

"OK, I do remember one. I knew a pilot from the 40th Bomb Group who were based on Tinian with us, over on West Field. His group were on a mission to Japan in the early part of 1945, I think it was. May or June. Other B-29 groups too. Five hundred bombers or so in all. Over Iwo Jima they picked up a fighter escort, 150 Mustangs. Near the coast of Japan, a storm from sea level to 25,000 feet moved in out of nowhere. The fighters and bombers had no choice but to go right through it. Due to a cross-up in communication, several flights of Mustangs turned back, while other flights pushed on. Fifty P-51s went through the front. Because of their weight and better stability in the air, the B-29s made it to the other side. Twenty-five of the fifty fighters didn't. No trace was found of any of them. Nothing! No bodies. No planes. No scraps of planes!"

"So... they hit a bad storm front," MacDonald replied. "Are you trying to say they went through a time barrier?"

"Maybe."

"I see. OK, getting back to the book you read, I would have to question the validity of what the pilot and co-pilot claimed to have seen. The rate of closure had to be at least 600 knots or thereabouts. That's pretty damn quick to make a solid identification."

Cameron shook his head, glancing over at Hulk and Tiger. "Those two were trained individuals. Your own pilots, here, I'm sure can establish a visual under the same circumstances. Don't you think so? It's their job."

"All right, I see what you mean. I'll give you that. Still, though–"

"Captain, I'm looking at this with a clear and open mind. So should you. I think I'm the only one here who has clearly come to grips with this. The *Mary Jane* and her crew have traveled through a time barrier, pure and simple. By the way, another incident in the book caught my attention."

"What?"

"Nobody really knew anything about the Bermuda Triangle either until after the war. It all hit the fan when those five US Navy Avenger torpedo bombers disappeared somewhere between Fort Lauderdale, Florida and the Bahamas on December 5, 1945. Six planes, plus a Martin Mariner search plane vanished! Twenty-seven men! The bombers' last radio messages were something to the effect that they were flying over several islands that according to their maps did not exist and that something was terribly wrong. The squadron flight leader didn't even know what direction they were flying. He said the ocean looked different to him. It was suggested by the author that the planes had gone back through time, when more islands had existed in that area. The search plane—the Mariner—was sent out and it never came back, either.

"Whatever is out there," Cameron went on, "is something beyond human comprehension. Call it a magnetic field, a black hole, or whatever. But it exists."

MacDonald shook his head. "I still can't believe this."

"I can, sir," Les said. "When I contacted the bomber, they called me Little Friend and wanted to know how many home runs Babe Ruth hit in 1927."

Cameron nodded, smiling. "Little Friend and Big Friend were terms we used in the war for fighters and bombers, and to tell if someone was American or not, we would ask baseball questions."

"I went alongside his port wing and he wanted to know what kind of aircraft I was flying."

"You mean he got a good look at you?" Cameron's eyes grew wide with surprise.

"He sure did. He wanted to know what I had. I told him an F-18 Hornet and added a smart crack like, 'Where've you been the last ten years?'"

Cameron chuckled. "This is fascinating. I have another crazy story for you. Back around ten years ago, I remember reading a book written by Martin Caiden, the air force writer. It was called *Fork-Tailed Devil: The P-38*. The epilogue of it went something like this. A flight of P-38 Lightnings left a North African base during the Second World War to take on some German fighters over the Mediterranean. Over the water, the battle started. When it came time to regroup and turn for home, the P-38 pilots realized that one of their boys was missing, but no one remembered him going down. Anyway, the flight returned to base. Hours later, he was finally reported missing in action, long after it was determined that he had to have run out of gas.

"So, two or three hours later, all of a sudden a P-38 appears over the base, engines roaring away. But before it could land, it fell apart without an explosion. Those at the base saw the pilot fall free, under an open parachute. The medics rushed to him. It was the missing pilot with a bullet in his head. He had been dead for hours, according to the doctors who examined him. Not only that, but when they found the gas tanks on the ground, they were dry. Bone dry! And had been bone dry for hours! The base CO found this whole thing so outlandish that he demanded and received the signatures of nearly 200 witnesses.

"*What happened*, you ask yourself? Did the pilot and P-38 go through some time warp? Perhaps. How can you account for it? Some hours were lost. That's for sure."

No one spoke for several seconds. "General Cameron?"

"Yes, Tiger."

"If the *Mary Jane* really has crossed the time barrier, wouldn't the crew realize it?"

"Not necessarily. As near as I can figure, what is hours to us is only minutes to them. They are not in our time for too long. Just long enough to be picked up on navy radar. Then they vanish. Why they are suddenly appearing here in 1990, I don't know. Maybe, the triangle holds the truth to these stories. As far as the crew is concerned, they're still in 1945 and flying the mission."

MacDonald had a question. "Assuming what you're saying is true, wouldn't they have clued in when they were in contact with Baker Two, whoever they were?"

"Probably not. Baker Two were the scientists on Iwo Jima. They weren't supposed to answer. Only listen."

"My callsign must have thrown them," Les grinned.

"What did you use?" Cameron asked.

"Zulu Two-Four-Three."

The general smiled. "No doubt. Under the old phonetic alphabet, we used Zebra for the letter Z." He exhaled heavily. "We have an alarming situation, nonetheless. The bomb—Fat Baby—is now armed. It is real, gentlemen. Let's accept it, and we'll all be better off. The quicker we realize it, the better. If this mission of theirs continues to its climax, then the *Mary Jane* could suddenly and without warning appear over Kyoto with an armed atomic bomb in her bomb bay. If the crew follows orders, they'll drop it on a defenseless city and kill a quarter of a million people. What day, we don't know."

MacDonald gulped at his coffee. "I still don't believe it."

"What time was the mission's H-Hour?" Les asked.

Cameron shrugged. "I don't remember. I was on Iwo with the scientists."

"Oh-seven-thirty," Robert answered.

Cameron looked over at his friend. "Oh, yeah. You were at the briefing."

"I just realized something, dad," Les said.

"What's that?"

"David lives in Kyoto. He's right in the line of fire."

Robert's eyes met his son's. "I know."

"OK, listen," MacDonald said. "Whether the *Mary Jane* has traveled through a time barrier or not–"

"It has," Cameron interrupted.

"We have to convince her to turn around," the navy captain continued.

"You bet, captain. The bomb is armed. We can't shoot her down." Cameron looked to his side. "Here comes the breakfasts."

"Sorry, gentlemen," the waitress apologized, blushing. "Your order was mixed up with someone else's."

Cameron grinned. "That's quite all right. We had a good, *long* talk."

Nine

Atop Nimitz Hill, Chief Petty Officer Richard Beatty had just come on duty at the NOCC—the Naval Oceanography Command Center/Joint Typhoon Warning Center. Standing near his desk, opposite a screen displaying a radar image of a cloud formation, he sipped his coffee and studied satellite photos of an area of the Pacific Ocean.

Beatty worked as a satellite analyst for an organization composed of 148 men—five civilians, 28 officers and 115 enlisted from within the air force and navy. The NOCC provided weather forecasts and environmental support for the Western Pacific and Indian Oceans, from the bottom of the oceans to the top of the atmosphere. This vast expanse covered forty million square miles, representing forty percent of the earth's ocean surface. The navy side of the JTWC—Beatty's section—furnished the Seventh Fleet of the US Navy and the civilian communities of Micronesia with typhoon alerts and other destructive weather early warnings. In addition to the satellite pictures, he and the others were involved in constant surveillance of the ocean areas, thanks to reports from air force and navy weather planes and ships, weather stations on the islands, and data fed to them from the navy's largest computer situated in Monterey, California.

The pictures in front of Beatty had been taken only minutes before via a satellite 22,000 miles above the earth and had been absorbed through a receiving unit, inside of which a sensitized film was developed and prints made. To untrained eyes, the cloud formations would not mean a thing. However, to Beatty, a particular spiral-shaped mass of clouds

73

300 miles in diameter north of the Gilbert Islands stood out. He had a pretty fair idea what was emerging out there.

Near or on the equator during this time of year, the ocean waters were quite warm. At least eighty degrees. The sun beat down day after day. Water vapor would condense and release its heat into the surrounding air. The air would start to rise and become warmer. As it warmed, it rose all the faster. Then it would pull in more moisture-laden air at sea level, which would rise and release more heat. Soon, a chain reaction would be set in motion, with destructive spiraling winds, huge cumulus clouds, strong rains, and a column of gently descending air in the middle. Add to this an easterly wave—a trough of low pressure—blowing from east to west in the inter-tropical convergence zone along the equator where the opposing winds of the two hemispheres meet, and a polar trough moving from west to east, and you had the makings of a serious tropical disturbance.

Beatty set his coffee cup down. Once he saw the eye of the disturbance, he arrived at only one conclusion.

A typhoon was beginning to spawn.

Mary Jane

At exactly 4:03 hours, the Superfortress navigator eyed his instrument panel from left to right—altimeter, compass, airspeed indicator, and clock. He pressed his intercom button and spoke clearly.

"NAVIGATOR TO COMMANDER. ALTER COMPASS HEADING TO THREE-TWO-TWO."

"TURNING THREE-TWO-TWO," a voice replied.

As the navigator jotted the necessary notations in his log, he felt the aircraft climbing in the darkness. The island of Iwo Jima was immediately below them. The original ETA he had given to the commander near Asuncion was only off by one minute. Not bad for two hours flying time.

In the cockpit, the pilot was calling out the altitude for the commander. "Seven thousand. . . Eight thousand. . ."

Once the commander reached the required 9,500 feet, he leveled off. "Take over will you, Carl," he said to his pilot.

"Sure."

"I'm going to make the rounds."

The commander—Ian Clayton—unstrapped himself from his seat

and stretched. Now he would begin the stroll to talk and to check in on each of the other eight crew members, starting with the tail gunner.

In its day, the Boeing B-29 Superfortress was a very unique bomber. To start, the pilot and co-pilot had different titles than was common with other World War Two bomber crews. Aboard the B-29, the pilot was actually called the commander. The co-pilot was the pilot. Many new features were inserted into the Superfortress. It had a pressurized crew compartment in the nose and a pressurized thirty-foot padded crawl tunnel over the huge bomb bay that led to a second pressurized cabin in the rear.

On the other B-29s, prior to the atomic missions, five computerized power-driven turrets were aboard where gunners could transfer control to each other. On the 509th bombers, this luxury was removed for the sake of speed and the weight of the atomic bomb, in this case the notorious Fat Baby, the 12,000-pound monster, twelve feet long and twenty-eight inches in diameter.

The bomb bay of every B-29 held a maximum of 20,000 pounds of conventional bombs. The four engines developed 2,200 horsepower each. The wingspan was a then unheard of 141 feet, and by the time it was loaded for a conventional bombing mission, the B-29 could carry an all up weight of 140,000 pounds. The B-29 altitude reached an impressive 31,000 feet. On March 9, 1945, three hundred B-29s wiped out fifteen square miles of Tokyo in a single incendiary. B-29s also dropped two deadly bombs on Hiroshima and Nagasaki. To the *Mary Jane* crew, the B-29 was the fiercest of all war machines. Most of the earlier bugs, such as engines overheating and catching fire in flight, and windows blowing out at high altitude, had now been dealt with. The *Mary Jane* crew had learned to cherish the B-29.

In the aft section, Clayton tapped his tail gunner. Sergeant Gabriel Schwartz was a skinny young man who had shot down three ME-109s over Europe with a Liberator squadron, prior to his arrival in the Pacific. In the tight compartment, he was adjusting his gun sight, which controlled a pair of .50-caliber machine guns. When he turned to greet the commander, Schwartz grinned. The small adjustable spotlight on the sight outlined his face and curly hair. Clayton liked him.

"Hi yuh, captain."

Clayton rested his hand on the lad's shoulder. "Keep a good eye out there, Gabe. You're the only eyes in the rear."

The gunner nodded. "I'll do my best."

"This will probably be the last mission anybody carries out in the war. Shoot down two more bogies and you're an ace."

"Fat chance of that," Schwartz laughed.

"You never know. Are you all set to take some good shots of the mushroom cloud?"

"You bet." Schwartz felt under his seat and yanked out a box camera. "It's not that great looking, but it gets the job done."

"Film all loaded up?"

"Ready to go, sir."

"Good man. See yuh."

"See yuh, captain."

Forward from the tail, the radar operator, Sergeant Mark Crosby, out of the corner of his eye saw Clayton open the bulkhead door. Crosby, the only married man aboard and one of the oldest too at twenty-five, was surrounded by mounds of equipment and instruments vital for the third atomic mission. Arranged on the shelves were direction finders, receivers, spectrum analyzers and decoders. His headset could receive different enemy frequencies in each ear. He would soon be listening for any enemy action, in addition to radar signals that could detonate the bomb before arriving at the target of Kyoto. Crosby was seated at his desk, smoking a cigarette, staring into his cylinder-shaped screen, when Clayton approached. The radar image—reflected radio waves that revealed the outlines of land masses—showed a small island passing directly underneath. With Crosby, Clayton peered into the screen to see the geographical image. When he pulled away, Crosby gave him the thumbs up.

The gunners' compartment behind the trailing edges of the wings was vacant for this trip, in order to keep the weight down. All the gun sights and armor plating had been removed, and the port and starboard blisters plus the central fire control position on top had been taken out and the holes smoothed over. Clayton stepped up to the tunnel opening and began his thirty-foot crawl. He emerged opposite the radio operator's desk, manned by Staff Sergeant Nevin Brown, an overweight, balding man in a creased baseball cap, reading a pocket book under a dim light. A big band music lover, he adjusted his headphones, gave the commander a wave, and returned to his reading. Diagonal to Brown was the meticulous navigator, Captain Dwight Marshall. He knew his job thoroughly and Clayton trusted the dark, handsome man with his life.

"Right on course, skipper," Marshall said over the drone of the four engines, calipers in hand. As usual, Marshall sat bent over his desk, where he had a Mercator map spread out. It was his job to guide the mighty B-29 over 1,500 miles of near-open water to the target of Kyoto and back to base again on the tiny island of Tinian. As navigational aids, he relied on dead reckoning (where course, speed, time and wind drift came into play), the star shots of celestial navigation, and reports from the radar navigator.

Across from Marshall sat another trusted crew member, the flight engineer, Sergeant Martin "Butch" Emerson, whose extra job on this mission consisted of helping the army explosives expert, an odd fellow by the name of Staff Sergeant Lawrence Ainsworth, known to the 509th as "Four Eyes."

Ainsworth was over forty, unmarried, and a vegetarian. He had very little hair, only tufts of red around his ears. He looked more like an absent-minded professor, or a bookworm, or a manager of a library in some out of the-way prairie town in South Dakota. His job, however, was one of the most important of all. He would perform the final arming of Fat Baby. Clayton glanced down at Four Eyes sitting against the bulk-head, who was still sweating from the work he had done on the bomb. Ainsworth didn't acknowledge Clayton at first because he was busy cleaning his glasses and probably couldn't see inside the compartment. When he put his thick glasses back on, he looked up into the eyes of the commander standing over him.

"You OK, sergeant? You look. . . flustered."

The navigator and radio operator exchanged glances, then stared at Ainsworth.

"Yes, captain," the sergeant replied quickly and clearly. "I'm fine. It was getting a little warm in the bomb bay."

To steady his nerves, Ainsworth turned and studied the bomb's control panel console just inches away from him. The console—thirty inches high by twenty inches wide—contained colored indicator lights, switches, and meters, and was attached to the bomb through the forward end of the bomb bay by a set of four cables, with twenty-four wires each. It was Ainsworth's job to monitor the console for any malfunction during the flight.

Clayton noticed a patch of powdery clouds drifting by through the Plexiglas nose as he made his way to the bombardier's station. Captain Paul Lunsford, a cool-as-ice twenty-year-old Californian who took his job seriously, was waiting. Seated, Lunsford had his hand resting on the Norden bomb sight's specially-constructed padded headrest, a device invented solely for the precise bombing accuracy of the atomic missions.

Glancing at the left side of the bombardier's control panel, located on the side wall to Lunsford's left, Clayton saw that the altimeter, remote reading compass, clock, and airspeed indicator all appeared to be functioning. On the right side were the bomb switches and warning lights.

"Don't worry," Lunsford announced with a grin. "I'll drop the bastard right on target."

Clayton smiled and turned in the direction of the cockpit. He tapped the pilot, the dark-skinned Carl Loran, on the shoulder. Loran gave the wheel back to the commander as he sat down. Loran was a young pilot—mid-twenties—from Minneapolis, cool and efficient. Got the job done. Clayton's type.

Clayton was a dedicated Superfortress pilot, one of the reasons Colonel Phil Cameron had hand-picked him for the third atomic mission. Like Cameron, he had flown B-17s in the European campaign, where the two had met, following a posting to the same squadron in Great Britain. Clayton's quick, perfectionist mind was a contrast to his slow-talking, Georgian drawl. On the ground, he was a good-natured individual, respected by his crew and others. But prior to every flight of the *Mary Jane*, Clayton became a different person. He'd take a trip to the bomber and hound the ground crew, making sure they checked everything. While they were busy working, Clayton would walk around the fuselage, pretending to see if any rivets were out of place and such, while out of the corner of his eye he would be watching the crew's every move. Then he'd ask the crew chief, Bob Shilling, things like whether the brakes were checked, and sometimes would even do some unnecessary manual labor himself on the B-29, much to Shilling's chagrin. To Shilling, Clayton was a *pain in the ass*.

Clayton didn't really enjoy flying. After three years in the Army Air

Forces, he treated it more or less as a job, a way to serve his country. He had wanted no part of the navy, the ground army, or the marines. Dropping a destructive plutonium bomb on Kyoto—the cultural capital of Japan—was part of that job. He was only obeying orders. He rationalized the mission the same way he had rationalized his way through his entire European tour of missions.

As far as he was concerned, he wasn't dropping bombs on people. He was dropping bombs on a point on a map.

Ten

GUAM

Inside his son's den, Robert Shilling flicked at the TV channel selector, while he and Phil Cameron leaned back in their comfortable chairs. Cameron was reading *Pacific Crossroads*, the local navy newspaper that was delivered free to every government home on the island. Les was on *Midway*. The women and kids were out shopping this cloudy Monday morning. Cameron and Robert had the house to themselves.

The two vets were both amazed to find that thirty-five cable TV channels serviced Guam. The Disney Channel, Country Music Television, The Movie Channel, and several Los Angeles stations flashed across the screen. Guam was no out-of-the-way post! Robert stopped at CNN, where a man was reading a weather report.

Cameron looked overtop his newspaper. "What's this, a storm?" he asked, curiously.

Robert turned the sound up.

The Typhoon Center on Guam, the TV man said, had been tracking a disturbance near the Gilbert Islands, two thousand miles from Guam. Although the system was moving slowly, a storm warning—an upgrade from a small-craft and gale warning where the winds were much lighter—had been issued for the Gilbert area.

"Two thousand miles away shouldn't be that big of a deal, should it, Phil?"

Cameron set his newspaper down on the stool. "It's close enough."

"Really?"

"Typhoons can actually be much more dangerous than Atlantic

hurricanes. Storms spawned in this area of the Pacific have no large land masses to break them up and can reach quite an intensity by the time they hit the more populated Marianas."

"You think we may be in trouble?"

"It's possible. Typhoons can travel at three to four hundred miles a day. Which means it could–"

"Be here in less than a week," Robert finished the sentence.

"Right. Providing it starts moving faster and builds strength over the open Pacific. So far, it hasn't. Yet. But, if it does, we are in the line of fire," Cameron concluded. "The Gilberts are southeast of here. The rotation of the earth causes spiraling storms to move northwest. Right smack where we are."

Robert looked gravely over at the former pilot, then fell back to his channel flicking. Cameron returned to his newspaper. Robert left the screen on the USA Network and rested his head on the back of the chair. Tired, he flicked the sound down and closed his eyes. Suddenly, for no reason, he thought of Tinian. He was half-dreaming, half-thinking. *Many years ago. August, 1945.* He was in the second row of a large tent, seated on a bench with his *Mary Jane* ground crew. In the front row were the aircrew. An expressionless army air force colonel in his forties walked into the room and stopped beside an easel covered by a black tarp. Those in the tent rose to their feet, then sat when he motioned them to do so.

It was coming back to Robert now. The briefing. The only air force briefing he was ever involved in. But this was no regular briefing. Then. . . the colonel began to speak.

"Good evening, men. My name is Colonel Mason. I've been sent here from Washington. The White House, to be exact. Tomorrow at oh-one-hundred hours, the crew of the MARY JANE"—his dark eyes set on Ian Clayton in the front row—"will take off on the most important mission of the war. Perhaps the most important ever. We still do not have any word from the Japanese following the first two atomic missions. Washington feels that they will not surrender. There-fore, the president himself has sent me here to advise you of one more strike with the most destructive atomic bomb of them all. The Manhat-tan Project scientists have assembled a plutonium bomb that we have named Fat Baby. When dropped, Fat Baby will kill close to a quarter of a million people."

The colonel then took a step back, grabbed a pointer, and pulled back the black tarp. It was a map. Five large letters stood out at the top of it.

KYOTO

Mason leaned on his pointer as if it were a pool cue.

"Yes, Kyoto. The shrine city of Japan. A million people. If we bomb Kyoto, then the Japs will know we mean business because this city is of little military importance. It will finally wake up the Jap hierarchy. Your aiming point will be the crossing of the"—his stick stabbed at two rivers in the north part of the city—"Kamo and Takano Rivers. Less than one mile southwest of this point is the Imperial Gardens. They will get a full blast of the bomb's power. Your initial point will be a series of shrines on the very west end of Lake Biwa to the east of Kyoto where a peninsula juts out. Surrounding this peninsula is a small community of scattered buildings called Otsu City. Time over target will be oh-seven-thirty."

The colonel flipped over to another map.

THE MARIANA ISLANDS

"You will maintain an altitude of 1,000 feet until Alamagen, then climb to 3,000 feet. At Agrihan, climb to 5,000 feet. Before you reach Iwo Jima, you will perform the first stage in arming the bomb. Over Iwo, you will climb to 9,500 and stay at that altitude until 400 miles from the Japanese coast, where the second and last stage in arming the bomb will be done. Your bombing altitude of 31,000 feet will then be reached. For this mission, you will go it alone. No spotters or weather aircraft. You're solo. If you are socked in by weather, do not bomb on radar. Turn back, disarm the bomb in the air, and drop her in the ocean. Acceptable weather for this mission will be a maximum of three-tenths cloud cover and favorable winds."

Mason reached for a pair of goggles from a nearby stand. "As with the other atomic missions, you must make sure your tinted goggles are covering your eyes once you are on the bomb run." He placed the pair over his eyes and demonstrated how, by turning a knob on the bridge of the nose, he could control the amount of light filtering through. "Before Fat Baby is dropped, adjust the setting to the lowest for maximum effect."

Mason removed the goggles. "There are a series of wires connected to the bomb. A steady tone will be heard in your earphones prior to the drop and will disappear once Fat Baby is gone. This is when the wires disconnect in the bomb bay. It's very important to make an immediate 155-degree turn at full throttle to get as far away from the shock waves as you can. The bomb has a barometric setting and will go off at 1,800 feet."

Mason stopped and stared at the crew who were to carry out the world's third atomic bombing mission. "Men, beware. If you have to bail out over Japan, you know the consequences. According to our intelligence sources, last month eight B-29 airmen were beheaded in Kobe before a large crowd of spectators. In flight, Captain Clayton will have in his possession nine cyanide capsules. One for each of you. It's your choice. If you are captured, give only your name, rank, and serial number."

Mason cleared his throat. "May God be with you."

Robert woke with a start, rubbed his eyes, and glanced over at Cameron. Robert sighed. Geez, forty-five years later the *Mary Jane* was still haunting him.

MARY JANE

At 05:30 hours, the top portion of the sun began to glow brightly above the horizon line to the east. It would soon be light. Two hours till H-Hour.

Staff Sergeant Nevin Brown set his book down on the table and ran through the radio frequencies until he heard some action. The signal was coming in strong through his headphones.

"BULLDOG, ZULU-TWO-FOUR-THREE AIRBORNE."

"ROGER ZULU TWO-FOUR-THREE, SWITCH TO BUTTON TEN."

"WILCO BULLDOG, SWITCHING TO TEN."

Brown sat straight up in his chair. Under the dim light, he searched through the range to pick up the frequency. What the hell was button ten? And what was Zulu Two-Four-Three and Bulldog? He scanned the frequencies frantically. Then. . . he caught something.

"RADIO OPERATOR TO COMMANDER," he contacted his superior.

"I HEAR YUH. WHAT'S UP?"

"SIR, LISTEN TO THIS SIGNAL I'VE PICKED UP."

"PIPE IT THROUGH."

"YES, SIR."

Brown hit a switch, and soon Clayton heard the conversation.

"BULLDOG TO ZULU TWO-FOUR-THREE. TARGET ON HEADING OF THREE-TWO-TWO. ANGELS NINE. ONE-NINETY KNOTS. RANGE, FOURTEEN MILES."

"ROGER BULLDOG. YOUR SIGNAL IS BREAKING UP."

"SWITCH TO BUTTON TWELVE, ZULU TWO-FOUR-THREE."

"ROGER."

Clayton let out a whistle. The heading of three-two-two was his heading. The speed and altitude were the same too.

Loran looked over at Clayton. "That's our Little Friend again. He must be based on Iwo."

"Yeah, I guess so."

Back in the radio room, Brown was playing through the dials. He stopped at another frequency, where he picked up a man's voice on a Japanese radio station.

"AND TO THOSE AMERICAN F-18 HORNET PILOTS AT THE MARINE CORPS AIR STATION IN IWAKUNI, WE HAVE BY REQUEST A REAL GOLDEN OLDIE OUT OF THE ARCHIVES. ROCK AROUND THE CLOCK BY BILL HALEY AND THE COMETS."

Stunned, Brown listened in his headset. What the hell! What American pilots on Iwakuni? F-18 Hornets! What were they? The announcer sounded American. Upstate New York or even Maine. Somewhere in New England for sure. Was he a prisoner of war? And that song. *Rock around the clock*. Never heard of it. Tokyo Rose wouldn't play a song like that. Big band music was her thing.

The song came on. . . and finished.

Brown continued to listen. The announcer came on again.

"THE PAUL MCCARTNEY TOKYO CONCERT IS NOW A SELLOUT. FOUR MONTHS BEFORE THE SHOW!"

Brown whipped his headset off. Had the guy gone screwy!

Eight miles behind the bomber, Les Shilling watched the B-29 form onto the radar screen. Closing quickly at 500 knots, Tiger was keeping pace with Les's Hornet off starboard.

Les hit the radio switch. "ZULU TWO-FOUR-THREE TO HAWKEYE THREE-SIX. ZULU TWO-FOUR-THREE TO HAWKEYE THREE-SIX."

Les heard the now familiar Georgian drawl. "I READ YOU, ZULU TWO-FOUR-THREE. BACK AGAIN, ARE YOU?"

"TURN BACK. YOUR MISSION IS AN ABORT. REPEAT, YOUR MISSION IS AN ABORT."

"THAT SO? WHO ARE YOU TO TELL US?"

Les was in visual range now with the B-29. "I KNOW EVERYTHING ABOUT YOUR MISSION. WHERE YOU CAME FROM. WHERE YOU'RE GOING AND WHAT YOU'RE CARRYING. TAKE FAT BABY BACK TO NORTH FIELD."

"I WANT THE CODENAME, ZULU TWO-FOUR-THREE."

What codename, Les thought, staring out at the *Mary Jane*.

Then the bomber disappeared.

The B-29 was now back in its own time. August 11, 1945.

Sergeant Mark Crosby chain-lit another cigarette and watched his radar screen, at the same time listening in on his special headset for the frequencies used by the enemy military controllers. Suddenly, he was startled to see the Japanese early-warning signal appear on the screen. It made three sweeps before locking onto the *Mary Jane*. In his headphones, Crosby heard the constant beep. That meant one thing. The Japs were tracking them. He heard a Jap controller talking down some fighters or bombers. He felt uneasy knowing that the enemy were on alert. But would they do anything about one lone target on their screens? He hoped not.

He pressed his throat mike. "RADAR TO COMMANDER."

"GO AHEAD."

"WE'RE IN RANGE. THE NIPS GOT A RADAR LOCK ON US."

"THANKS."

Ainsworth stood up from his leaning position against the bulkhead inside the radio room and walked through the bomb bay hatch. He had gone there by himself this time. The unheated bomb bay was a pleasant seventeen degrees centigrade. He could do the last operation in comfort before the B-29 climbed to bombing altitude. Because he had only a small job to perform on the bomb this time, the flight engineer was not needed as an assistant.

Ainsworth eased along the catwalk, so nervous that his hands were shaking. According to the mission plan, he was to replace the green plugs with the red ones that he was carrying. But he didn't. He deliberately left the green plugs in the bomb. He waited for exactly four minutes, sweating all the more, then returned to the radio compartment.

Ainsworth nodded at Brown, who hit the intercom. "RADIO TO COMMANDER. THAT'S IT, SIR. IT'S READY."

In the cockpit, Clayton smiled coldly at his pilot. "COMMANDER TO CREW. FAT BABY IS NOW FULLY ARMED. THE NIPS ARE TRACKING US. HOPEFULLY, THEY WON'T DO A THING. WE'RE ONLY ONE. WE ARE NOW NINETY MINUTES FROM THE ENEMY COAST. PREPARE FOR A CLIMB TO 31,000 FEET. OVER."

Eleven

Inside the "Storm Room" on Nimitz Hill, Chief Petty Officer Richard Beatty called his commanding officer—Captain Raymond Carruthers—on a local line.

"Captain, it's Beatty. I have the shots, sir."

"Stay there. I'll be right over."

Over strong coffee, the two men studied recent satellite photos of the storm that was now reaching typhoon status and tagged Tropical Storm Matilda. The infra pictures showed a twisting mass of clouds over the Caroline Islands, almost 1,500 miles southeast of Guam. The two realized that although Matilda was still a long way off, typhoons had a nasty habit of fueling themselves over all that open water, building up a destructive path as they swung west.

"It's moving our way, captain."

"So it is," Carruthers agreed.

An ensign walked up and handed Carruthers a report just received by radio from a typhoon hunter aircraft that was at that moment in the eye of the storm. The aircraft was a flying laboratory, crammed with instruments that collected all forms of data related to the weather disturbance. The report gave vital information such as the storm's size, location, temperature, moisture content, along with its speed, course, and maximum winds.

"Winds eighty-five knots," Carruthers observed. "We got ourselves a whopper. It's official now. Typhoon Matilda. Issue the appropriate typhoon warnings and watches for the Caroline Islands."

"Yes, sir."

One piece of data, in particular, startled Captain Carruthers. It was the aneroid barometric pressure reading, which recorded atmospheric pressure. He knew that the lower the setting, the worse the storm. Normally, a sea-level reading should register somewhere in the neighborhood of twenty-nine to thirty inches. The typhoon hunter registered a reading of 26.55, one of the lowest ever recorded in the Pacific.

When Robert Shilling and Phil Cameron arrived at Agana Naval Air Station, Captain MacDonald was already waiting for them by a MH-53E Super Stallion helicopter on one of the dispersal tracks. The sun was setting. Over the loud whir of the blades, the captain shook hands with the two war vets, then motioned them to step through the sliding door on the side.

Once inside the back of the empty cargo area, door closed, MacDonald filled the two in on the latest events as they sat inside the bulkhead that separated the cabin. They each put on a helmet and life vest and buckled up their seat belts.

"We got some trouble. Big trouble. As I said over the phone, we're going to *Midway*. I see you're each wearing a windbreaker and that you brought along a night bag. Good."

"What are we up against now?" Cameron wanted to know.

MacDonald held up his hand to Cameron to curtail further questions. "First things first. I owe you an apology, general."

"You do?"

"Yes. I'm convinced now that time travel is no theory. Les and Tiger said they saw the *Mary Jane* vanish in mid-air, and I believe them. They were less than a mile behind her."

Cameron merely smiled.

The captain rubbed his chin and continued. "Now, *Mary Jane* was last sighted 325 miles off the coast of Japan. Your son, Mr. Shilling, ordered the bomber to turn back. They refused. They—Clayton and his crew—insisted that they needed the codename for the mission to do that. Do either of you know it?"

Cameron shrugged, followed by Robert.

"Don't you know it, general? You were the commanding officer of the 509th!"

"I was never given it."

"Why not?"

"I was on Iwo Jima at the time with the scientists. Only the crew, the briefing officer, and a few selected others knew it. Seeing that it was a solo mission, the understanding was that the fewer who knew, the better. Security."

"Security, is right. I attended the briefing," Robert confirmed.

"That's right. Your ground crew *was* there. Well?" Cameron asked, waiting for a reply.

"We were ordered to leave at one part of the briefing. And you guessed it, when the codename was given out."

"Great!" Macdonald said. "One of our options now is to shoot it down."

Cameron didn't like that. "With an armed nuclear bomb? Are you serious?"

"It's an option, general."

"Try another one?"

The engine and rotor noise rose as the helicopter began to lift, making conversation difficult.

"That's why you two are here. On *Midway*, we will make radio contact with the *Mary Jane*. One of you or both may have to convince Captain Clayton to turn the bird around."

Cameron frowned. "Without the codename? I don't think so."

"Try, please. You have to. Think hard and recall anything you can about these men, things that only they and you will know. Where they came from. Anything you know about them prior to joining the 509th. Anything! Everything!"

"I see," Cameron acknowledged. "For instance, Clayton and I flew B-17s with the same squadron based in England. I remember his machine. It too was the *Mary Jane*."

"By the way, who was Mary Jane, anyway?" Robert asked.

Cameron thought for a moment. "His girl back in Georgia. He always said she was built like a brick shit house."

"Now we're getting somewhere," MacDonald said, encouraged.

"I have a question, captain," Robert said.

"Go ahead, Mr. Shilling."

"Don't you think the brass aboard *Midway* will have to be filled in on this—the flight of the *Mary Jane*?"

"I know, I know," MacDonald replied.

The helicopter pulled away from the base. The three men waited until the whirring machine was a thousand feet over the water and the engines were set at their cruising speed of 150 knots before anyone spoke again.

"How long will we be in the air?" Robert asked.

MacDonald checked his watch. "Let's see. *Midway* is 1,100 nautical miles to the north. At cruising speed, we should be there in approximately seven hours, after allowing a brief stop on Iwo Jima to refuel."

Cameron and Robert exchanged curious glances. Neither felt comfortable being away at such a time.

"We could be gone a few days?"

"That's right, general. But we'll try to wrap this up as quickly as we can."

"I hope so. Our wives are back on Guam, and there's a typhoon warning for the Carolines."

"I know," MacDonald nodded. "I'll keep in touch with the typhoon center for reports. The latest is that if it does hit Guam, it won't be until the end of the week."

"If we can't talk Clayton down, then we blow the *Mary Jane* out of the sky, that right? You don't think nuclear explosion is kind of risky?"

"Given the circumstances, general, we have no choice but to do it, after all else fails. We could get away with it over water before she reaches the coast. The F-18 Hornet is equipped with Sparrow AIM-7 radar-guided missiles with a range of thirty miles. That leaves plenty of room for Tiger and Hulk to stay clear of debris and any shock waves."

"I hope it doesn't have to come to that."

MacDonald gave the two a despairing stare. The copter hit an air pocket, shaking the men. "I hope it doesn't either."

Kyoto

David picked up Toshika in front of her apartment building. She got into his Porsche and closed the passenger door with a firm slam. David greeted her with a light kiss on the lips.

"Thanks for coming," she said. "I appreciate it."

"No problem." David put the sports car in gear and sped away in the night. "I'd like to meet your family friend. What did you say his name was?"

"Paul Mason. Colonel Paul Mason." Toshika looked at him with concern. "I should warn you. The colonel's mind isn't always clear. Last time I saw him he didn't even remember me. But, you know, he's in his nineties."

"So, how did your family get to know him in the first place?"

"After the war he quit the air force, moved to Japan and invested in Mitsubishi, the same company my father worked for."

"Big company. He must be a rich man."

"He is, and his kids and grandchildren are out to get his millions."

David drove through the northern suburbs of Kyoto, over a bridge that spanned the Kamo River, past the beautiful Kyoto Botanical Gardens. A mile beyond, he slowed at a sprawling one-story building nestled inside a cluster of neatly-trimmed trees. He pulled into the parking lot near the lobby.

Following Toshika down an empty corridor, David was led to a room near the kitchen. Inside was a pale, thin, wrinkled old man in a wheelchair. He was dressed in a nightshirt and appeared to be staring out through the long, wide window at the slowly setting sun. Toshika approached the man slowly, so as not to startle him. As she got closer, he turned to her.

"Hello, colonel," she said loudly, keeping in mind that he was hard of hearing.

The old man smiled. "Oh, yes, Toshika." He stuck a bony hand out for her to touch. His voice was rough. "My daughter just left. Did you see her?"

"No, I didn't, colonel." Toshika didn't know if she really had been there or if he was imagining it. But at least he had recognized her today. That didn't occur too often. "I brought a friend with me."

"Who?"

"David Shilling."

The colonel held out his hand and David shook it lightly. The old man looked pleased.

"Would you like to watch some TV?" Toshika asked.

"Yes, I would like that."

Toshika positioned herself behind the old man, gripped the handles to the wheelchair and went through the door, David walking alongside.

There were others in the large TV room, two old women and three visitors in their thirties. They were all glued to a news bulletin on Typhoon Matilda. David and Toshika pulled up chairs on either side of the colonel in one far corner, facing the TV set.

"He likes it when he hears about old times. We may be in luck. It sounds like he might remember a few things today," she whispered to David.

Toshika carried on some family small talk for fifteen minutes with the colonel, who remembered her father and asked how he was doing. After she ran out of things to discuss, she glanced at David.

"Colonel," David began, "I hear you were with the air force during World War Two."

The man's eyes brightened for a moment. "Yes, I was."

"David's father flew B-29s," Toshika interrupted.

The colonel turned to David.

"He didn't fly them, actually, he worked on them," David continued. "He was ground crew."

Raising his finger, the old man tried to find the words. "What was your father's squadron?"

"The 509th Composite Group."

"What?"

"You'll have to speak louder," Toshika advised.

"The 509th Composite!"

The colonel's face sparkled. "I did some work for them. Yes, I did. They dropped the atomic bombs, you know."

"That's right, sir, they did." David paused. "You were with the 509th?"

"Yes."

Toshika smiled at David. She hadn't seen the colonel this attentive in weeks.

"Which aircraft was your father's? Did it have a name?"

"It sure did. The *Mary Jane*."

The colonel's mouth dropped open in shock.

"Colonel, are you all right?" Toshika wanted to know.

"The *Mary Jane* had a bomb, too," the colonel said. "A big bomb."

"It did." That was news to David. "What kind of bomb?"

"Plutonium."

David cleared his throat. He looked at the others in the room. No one seemed to be paying attention to them. *What was going on here?* "Plutonium? You mean it carried an atomic bomb?"

Toshika nudged David with her elbow. "Don't take to heart everything he tells you. He makes up stories."

"Yeah, but, did you see his face light up when I mentioned the name of my father's bomber?"

"So?"

"Colonel, are you sure it was carrying an atomic bomb?"

The man nodded, as if he understood the question perfectly.

David was flabbergasted. He remembered his father once making reference to the fact that his B-29 had disappeared on a routine mission to Japan only days before the Japanese surrender. Could this senile old man really be telling the truth about *Mary Jane*? But who was this colonel? And how would he be privy to such information?

"Sir, what did you do with the 509th?"

The colonel leaned forward. "What?"

"What did you do with the 509th?"

"Intelligence."

"Intelligence?" David shot a glance to Toshika. Even she was surprised.

"I wouldn't necessarily believe all this," she warned David.

"Why not?" He turned to the old man. "How do you know all this about the *Mary Jane*?"

Just then an elderly nurse in stark white walked into the room to announce that visiting hours were over.

"How do you know all this stuff, colonel?" David asked again.

The colonel waved his bony hand in the air. "I know all about it. Big hush-hush."

David felt every nerve in him tingle. "What was the target?"

The nurse was now standing over the three of them. She started to take hold of the wheelchair's handlebars. "Sir, ma'am, visiting hours are over."

"You'd better listen to her, David. They're strict about visiting hours."

Looking up to the woman in white, he said, "Sure. Sorry. May I wheel him back in?"

"I don't see why not."

"Thank you."

David and Toshika took the colonel down the hall. The nurse went into the room first, enabling David to stop the wheelchair by the entrance, giving him time for one last try.

"Colonel," he asked one more time, "what was the *Mary Jane*'s target?"

The old man's face grew hard. He motioned with his finger for David to bend down. David moved his head so that his left ear was only inches away from the colonel's lips.

"Right here, mister," the colonel whispered softly and clearly. "Kyoto."

Driving back to Toshika's apartment, David rammed through the gears of his car.

"So, the *Mary Jane* was actually on an atomic mission. What do you know?"

Toshika laughed, shaking her head. "Like I said before, he makes stories up. I never know what to believe. Sometimes he recognizes me, sometimes he doesn't. Look, he doesn't know what he's talking about. There were only two atomic missions. Hiroshima and Nagasaki. That's it!"

"But why would he make the story up?"

"He's old. He's imagining it."

"What if he's telling the truth? He said my father's crew was on an atomic mission. My father told my brother and me that the *Mary Jane* was lost on a routine bombing mission to Japan. It disappeared and was never heard from again. Plane and crew. Come to think of it, we always got the feeling that dad was hiding something from us, that we weren't getting the whole truth. Now this. What if my father's bomber really was on an atomic raid? Geez!"

Toshika shook her head. "What difference does it make now?"

"It means a helluva lot to me. What if the *Mary Jane* was out on an atomic mission—the third atomic mission—and something went wrong along the way? What if it ran into mechanical trouble? She could have crashed into the Pacific. The colonel said it was a big hush-hush. The mission had probably started but it never succeeded." David shrugged his shoulders. "The war ended soon after, anyway. So, they kept it all a secret. A big *hush-hush*."

"That's if you can believe the colonel."

"I think I do."

"Oh, come on, David! It would have been recorded in the history books somewhere."

"But if something did go wrong and it didn't get to the target, why would it be in the history books? Because it failed. Maybe the bomb detonated prematurely over the water. It could have been shot down by a fighter. Or ground guns. Anything."

"OK," Toshika sighed, "let's say it did happen. Why a third atomic mission?"

"According to the history books, your government didn't surrender right after the Nagasaki mission. Maybe the United States were ready with a third bomb, and the target was Kyoto."

Toshika sighed. "If you say so. But I still don't think so."

"I'm going to check into it."

"Really. What are you going to do?"

"You'll see."

At home, David went to his den and sat by the phone, while running the meeting with Colonel Mason through his mind one more time. What if the *Mary Jane* really was on an atomic mission? What a blockbuster! Had his father known this? What a coincidence bumping into Mason. Providing he was telling the truth.

David tapped a number on his phone and waited until he heard a woman's voice on the other end.

"Hello."

"*Gail?* It's David."

"I'm sorry, this isn't Gail. But I'll get her for you."

"Thank you." Who was that? David wondered. He detected a French accent.

"Hello."

"Gail?"

"Yes."

"It's David."

"Hi, David. What's up? How yuh doing?"

"Good. Who was that who answered?"

"General Cameron's wife."

"You mean *the* General Cameron? Phil Cameron, the Hiroshima pilot?"

"The same one."

Everywhere David turned today, it seemed the past was there. "Why is General Cameron's wife at your house?"

"The Camerons are visiting us for a few days. It seems your father knows the general quite well."

"Is that so." David was learning new things about his dad by the minute. "So, dad is friends with General Cameron."

"Seems so."

"Anyway, listen, is dad there? I need to talk to him."

"Nope."

"Will he be back soon?"

"Not for a couple days."

Then David realized that Cameron would probably know the story behind the *Mary Jane*. But would he talk. "Is General Cameron there?"

"He's gone, too."

Catching a strange tone to Gail's voice, David continued. "Where are they? I need to reach dad. . . both of them. It's important."

"How important?"

"Very important. What is this?"

"I'm not supposed to say where they are unless it's important."

"Where are they, Gail? I need to reach them immediately."

"They're out to sea on USS *Midway*."

"You're putting me on!"

"Not at all. It's official US Navy business."

"OK, then, is Les around?"

"He's out to sea, too."

Annoyed, David sighed and rubbed his face. "Listen to me carefully, Gail. Can you relay a message to dad for me? It's an emergency."

"Yeah, I can do that."

"You'll have to jot it down word for word."

"Hold on." There was rustling on the other end. "OK, I got a pen and paper. Shoot."

Twelve

USS MIDWAY

USS *Midway* was built in the last year of the Second World War. Designated CV-41, she was an old carrier, as far as active carriers went. She and the equally-old USS *Coral Sea* were the only two carriers that formed the Midway Class in the modern US Navy.

Midway had many things going against her. She displaced less tonnage than the other carriers, at 62,000 tons full load, compared to at least 80,000 tons for the others. Not only that, she was shorter in length and flight-deck width. While the other classes were over 1,000 feet in length with at least 252 feet of flight-deck width, *Midway*'s specs were 979 and 238, respectively. *Midway* also held fewer aircraft, seventy-five compared to around ninety, and fewer men, just under 3,000 compared to over 3,000 for the other classes. She had been home-ported in Yokosuka, Japan, since 1973. This year, she was celebrating her forty-fifth anniversary. Despite her advanced age, she was ready to deploy to the Indian and Pacific Oceans on very short notice. She could still hold her own if and when the crunch came.

After midnight, Robert Shilling caught a great view of *Midway* through the porthole of the Super Stallion. He was tired and on the verge of being sick to his stomach from the bumpy, six-hour-plus flight across the water and was anxious to set foot on the carrier now below and to the side of him. A half mile from touchdown, the copter pilot throttled back to 130 knots and cruised at that speed until 100 feet off the deck, where he dropped down to 30 knots.

The touchdown point was marked with flashing strobe lights. The

LSO waved the helicopter down, while the pilot watched the mirrored approach carefully, the same landing device used by the fighter pilots during their recoveries. The Stallion pilot hit the deck a little too hard, giving the passengers a jolt. Ground crewmen outside rushed to secure the landing gear with restraining cables. One of the men motioned the pilot to cut the power. The engine noise and large whirling propeller slowed down and stopped.

Inside, Shilling was the last one to release his safety belt, Mae West and helmet. He followed Cameron and MacDonald through the side door and onto the deck. A strong, cool wind in the 30-knot range hit his back. In the darkness, he saw the outlines of *Midway*'s Air Wing, several tightly parked F-18 Hornets, wings folded and safely stowed. He was excited at being aboard his first US Navy carrier, the same carrier that his son had called home many times.

A tall officer with a round face greeted the three men, first with a salute to Agana's CO. "Captain MacDonald, welcome to *Midway*. I'm the executive officer, Commander Vince Digano. Let me take you and your guests to Commodore Prentice." Digano glanced up to the super-structure behind him. He was known as the XO, the ship's president, the CO's deputy, which meant he was Prentice's mouthpiece, the man who did all the yelling at the department heads. He was the man who got things done. Some nicknamed him the Headhunter.

"Thank you," MacDonald replied. "Lead the way."

"Follow me, sir."

The recently-promoted Commodore William Prentice was waiting for the visitors on the bridge. He was seated in his upholstered chair to the port side of a large rectangular glass. From this position, he had a bird's-eye view of the entire carrier deck. The ship had just finished a series of night launches and recoveries only thirty minutes before the arrival of the Super Stallion, with Prentice watching the entire opera-tion from his perch. Some officers and NCO's were with him now in the room full of electronic and computerized systems and consoles.

Prentice was considered a hard-liner, a stickler for precision and detail. The sailors weren't that crazy about him, but he had a good rapport with his officers. He knew how to get the best out of them with-out stretching them beyond their limits. He was a fit man of medium height, with a rugged dark-brown complexion and black hair. He wore glasses over icy grey eyes. Along his left cheek ran a long scar, a souvenir from a barroom brawl in San Diego twenty years earlier, where he was jumped on by three civilians. MacDonald—a young fellow officer he didn't know at the time—had come to his rescue. From then on, Prentice and MacDonald were friends for life. Prentice to this day still felt he *owed* MacDonald one.

Prentice walked over to his friend and shook his hand. "It's great to see you again. It's been a while. What, two years?"

"Yeah, I think so."

"So, who are your guests and what's so damn important enough to bring you all the way out here?"

"Will—Commodore Prentice," MacDonald corrected himself, "I'd like you to meet Major-General Phillip Cameron retired, United States Air Force."

Prentice blinked. "General Cameron. It's a pleasure. I *thought* you looked familiar. Welcome."

"Thank you," Cameron answered. "Quite the flat-top, commodore, for one that dates back to the end of the Second World War."

"It's still of use to the grand old navy. If our pilots can land on her, then they can land on the bigger ones. The Old Gray Lady can still perform."

"And," MacDonald continued, "this is Lieutenant Les Shilling's father, Robert Shilling. Incidentally, he was ground crew with the General's old war outfit on Tinian, the 509th Composite Group."

"Is that so? Pleased to meet you, Mr. Shilling. Another pleasure."

"The pleasure is all mine, sir," Robert said, holding out his hand, glancing at the commodore's spotless working khaki uniform and officer's cap. "Thank you for allowing a land lover like myself the privilege of seeing your ship."

"No problem at all." The commodore's handshake was as strong as a steel vice grip. "Mr. Shilling, I'd like to say to you that your son is one of the finest, most dedicated pilots in the whole US Navy. He's a credit to the uniform he wears. And I compliment you in the raising of such a fine son."

The words caught Robert off guard. He was suddenly proud—very proud—of his son. Obviously, Prentice meant everything he said. "He's a good boy."

Looking around the room, before resting his eyes on his old friend,

MacDonald said, "Will, we need to talk. And I think we should include Hulk and Tiger."

"Sure, George. Let's go to my office."

Minutes later, inside the small office, Prentice waited for Les and Jack Runsted to arrive before he said, "OK, let's have it. What's this all about?"

MacDonald told the incredible story of the *Mary Jane* in a precise step-by-step manner. Every so often, the others in the office broke in to confirm certain portions of the crazy tale. Prentice sat, arms folded.

When MacDonald finished, Prentice said as calmly as he could, "I don't know whether to laugh, cry, or have all four of you thrown in the looney bin."

"I know it sounds bizarre, Will, but what else can we say? The *Mary Jane* has slipped through the time barrier."

Prentice twiddled his thumbs, then uttered, "Relax. I believe you. I think. Anyway, this message I received from Agana might have something to do with whatever we're dealing with. Mr. Shilling, it's for you." The commodore pulled out a single piece of typed copy from under a file on his desk and handed it to Robert. "You might as well read it out loud."

Robert did.

ROBERT SHILLING USS MIDWAY 2205 HOURS AUG 28. JUST MET COLONEL PAUL MASON IN KYOTO. HE TOLD ME ABOUT THE MARY JANE'S MISSION. PLEASE CONFIRM. DAVID.

"Mason?" Cameron said. "I didn't think he was still alive. He's got to be in his nineties."

"Who's this Mason?" Prentice asked.

Glancing at the sheet, then looking squarely at the commodore, Cameron said, "He gave the briefing for the third atomic mission."

"Oh. So, how did your son happen to come across Colonel Mason?"

Robert shrugged. "I honestly don't have a clue. But–"

"He must know the codename for the Kyoto mission," Les said.

"You're right, son. Exactly what I was going to say."

"According to the pattern of these sightings," the commodore said, "you must suspect that the B-29 will be spotted again. Soon. Correct?"

"You bet, Will. We need your help."

"You got it."

"Thanks."

"OK, this is what we do. Mr. Shilling," Prentice said, turning to Robert, "we'll send a priority message to your son in Kyoto. He *has* to—he must—get the codename."

"What if we don't get it?" Les interrupted. "If the old guy's in his nineties, he might not remember. Do we have another option?"

Cameron smiled grimly. "We might have to blow the *Mary Jane* out of the sky before it reaches the Japanese coast."

"What if we don't catch up to her again until she's over the mainland?" Runsted asked. "Then what, sir?"

"Then, we'll have to talk her down," Cameron answered. "We'll have to prove to the pilot who we really are. I'm sure Robert and I can recall certain things here and there that only the pilot, and Bob, and myself were familiar with."

The commodore cleared his throat. "OK, listen. So far, only the five of us know about this whole damn thing, right?" The others nodded. "Of course, there will be a few members of my ship who will have to be briefed on the situation."

MacDonald folded his arms. "We expected that. You know your personnel. We'll leave the chosen few up to you."

Prentice nodded, looking down at his desk. "All those aboard the bridge, the officer of the deck, the exec officer. Let's see, the operations officer, the communications officer. . . and the CAG."

"Are you sure that's enough," MacDonald chuckled.

Everyone laughed.

"OK, I'll get off that priority dispatch to your son, Mr. Shilling," Prentice said. "Then. . . we sit tight and wait."

Kyoto

David was in the middle of a deep sleep when his Japanese butler knocked on his bedroom door. "Mister Shilling. Mister Shilling." He had to enter the room and shake his employer several times before he woke up.

"What? What's the matter?"

"Mr. Shilling, a young man from the US Navy Department is at the door."

"What!" David rubbed his face. "He is? What for?"

"I don't know, sir. He said it's urgent."

David swallowed hard and glanced at the digital clock radio on his nightstand. *Geez, five-fifteen.* He raised himself to one elbow. It took him another moment or two to realize it must've had something to do with the message he had sent his father. *What was the hurry?* "Tell him I'll be right there. Just let me throw a robe on."

"Yes, sir."

A minute later, David stumbled his way to the entrance to meet the young officer in blue who was waiting inside the door. Clutched in his hand was a sealed white envelope. "Mr. David Shilling?"

"That's me." David squinted into the hall light. "What can I do for you?"

"I have a priority message for you, sir. I have orders to see that you open this letter, read it, and act upon it immediately. We are to meet a Colonel Paul Mason. I will accompany you, sir."

"Really now. At five in the morning?"

"Yes, sir."

The officer handed David the envelope, who tore it open to find the typed words on official US Navy stationery.

DAVID SHILLING 0225 HOURS AUG 29. YOUR FATHER RECEIVED
MESSAGE REGARDING MASON. DO NOT DELAY. FIND THE CODE-
NAME FOR THE KYOTO MISSION.
COMMODORE PRENTICE USS MIDWAY.

David held the paper in his hand, staring ahead, thinking it through. Apparently, there really was a Kyoto mission. And *Midway*'s CO had his fingers in on it, too. Why?

"Sir," the officer said, "I will wait while you get dressed. Transportation is provided."

"I'll be right with you."

In less than ten minutes, David was dressed and met the officer in the navy staff car in the driveway. David gave directions and the officer drove several miles per hour over the speed limit in the light traffic to the retirement home on the other side of the city. They went to the front office, where they were met by a pretty Japanese nurse.

"Yes?"

"I know it's early, ma'am. But this is official United States Navy business. May we see Colonel Paul Mason, please? It's urgent."

The nurse smiled at the young man in uniform. "If you can wait another half hour, Ensign–"

"Walker, ma'am. Ensign Walker."

"Please, wait another half hour. He's still sleeping. But he usually rises earlier than the others."

"But I have orders–"

"That'll be fine, ma'am," David interrupted, touching the ensign's shoulder. "We'll wait. Let us know as soon as he's awake, please."

"I promise."

"Thank you." He turned to the officer. "Let's take a seat, ensign."

The two found chairs in the nearby vacant lobby.

"Take 'er cool, Walker," David said. "Mason is closing in on a hundred. We better get him at his best. OK?"

The officer removed his cap and held it. "Yes, sir."

"Tell me, Walker, why the great urgency here?"

"Sir?"

"What's the damn big hurry?"

"I can't tell you that because I don't know."

"Well, can you tell me what you do next?"

"Next?"

"Come on, after we talk to Mason? What were you told, anyway?"

The officer leaned forward and lowered his voice. "Sir, you are to obtain a codename for what is termed the Kyoto Mission. I am to relay this codename—pronto—to USS *Midway* on the open sea via my base on Yokosuka."

"I see. So, did they brief you on the *Mary Jane* too?"

"What's the *Mary Jane*?"

David smiled. "You'll soon find out. Just stick around."

"I intend to."

"By the way, how's your World War Two history, Walker?"

USS MIDWAY

Commander Digano took Cameron and Robert to the hangar bay, down two steep flights of stairs, and down a hall to the cabin that the two would be sharing. Digano left promptly.

"Upper or lower bunk, Bob?" Cameron joked.

"Well, general, you outrank me. Your choice."

"In that case, I'll take the upper."

The two tired men dropped their night bags on the floor. Cameron immediately climbed up to his bunk and laid down. In minutes, he was fast asleep in spite of the bright overhead light. Robert used the adjoining washroom and when he came back he turned the main light off and turned on a small desk lamp in one corner. He sat on the edge of the bunk, checking the cabin out. It was windowless, constructed of gray steel, with two dressers to one side, a chair, a desk, and a large closet along one full wall. He opened the closet and found a collection of half-dozen sweaters, some slacks, and flight jackets. In one dresser he found shirts, underwear, and work boots. The other dresser had the same for Cameron. Robert smiled. The navy were looking after them. First class all the way.

Reaching for his night bag, Robert pulled out a small hardcover book he had come across in his son's library only minutes before leaving for Agana Naval Air Station. He studied the cover which was a black and white picture of the 1945 atomic explosion over Hiroshima snapped from General Cameron's bomber. Robert thumbed through the book until he came to photos of some Japanese atomic casualties. The pictures were horrible. Robert knew that. Women. Children. Scars. Skin falling off. As far as he was concerned, it was unfortunate so many people had to suffer for their government's misguided aggressive motives. They had started it at Pearl Harbor, one well-placed torpedo alone entombing over 1,000 men in the USS *Arizona*. What was worse?

Robert flipped through the book and began to read the results of the first atomic blast forty-five years ago. The bomb had exploded at 1,890 feet. The temperature at ground zero was several thousand degrees centigrade, with the core of the fireball reaching fifty million degrees centigrade. The blast burned the skin of people two miles away. Eighty thousand of Hiroshima's 320,000 residents died instantly or were severely wounded. Sixty thousand buildings were destroyed. Bodies were vaporized. Of the city's 200 doctors, 180 were soon dead or injured; 1,650 of 1,780 nurses were in the same state. The heat transferred the black lettering from books and newspapers onto skin and clothing. The patterns of caps and clothing were imprinted on bodies. Socks were burned onto legs.

Robert put the book down and turned out the light. He undressed and climbed into the bunk. It had taken the book to emphasize the magnitude of the destruction. Now, the *Mary Jane* was carrying a plutonium bomb that would make the Hiroshima blast look like a fart by comparison. It had hit home. Damn it all to hell, his son David was right in the line of fire.

He shook his head. And this was supposed to be a vacation!

MARY JANE

Staff Sergeant Nevin Brown zipped through the radio frequencies to find his favorite gal, *Tokyo Rose.*

He stopped at a Glenn Miller tune, *Tuxedo Junction.* He found it. Now there was some familiar music. Not that other stuff. Haley's Comets or whatever they were called. He listen until the song finished, then Tokyo Rose spoke in her soothing propaganda voice that never ceased to "thrill" the Americans stationed in the Pacific. Brown listened in only to catch the American big band selections she played.

> "WELL BOYS, I DO HOPE YOU'RE ENJOYING THE GLENN MILLER MUSIC I'VE BEEN PLAYING FOR YOUR LISTENING PLEASURE. DOESN'T BIG BAND MUSIC REMIND YOU A WHOLE LOT OF HOME? IT SHOULD. TUXEDO JUNCTION, THE CHATTANOOGA CHOO CHOO, KALAMAZOO. THAT'S WHERE YOU SHOULD BE RIGHT NOW, BOYS. BACK IN THE US OF A. THERE'S STILL A LOT OF FIGHT LEFT IN THE IMPERIAL FORCES OF JAPAN. WE DON'T SCARE EASY."

Brown shut the radio off and chuckled to himself. Who was the bitch trying to kid? Japan fight? After two atomic bombs? Wait till they get a load of the *Mary Jane. An honest-to-goodness bomb load.*

USS MIDWAY

After only three hours of sleep, Robert and Cameron were wakened and told by Commander Digano that they'd be taken on a short tour of the carrier. Twice below deck, Digano had to stop and speak into his headphones. Then he continued to lead the men outside.

On the flight deck the two Hornets belonging to Les and Tiger had already been towed into position on Number One and Number Two catapults. To Robert, the deck seemed so huge. . . and never ending. He could hear the ocean fizzing and hissing below. The air stung from a mixture of salt and jet fuel. He saw the ocean horizon line, complete with white caps, superimposed on low clouds. The wind was cool, the sky bright and sunny to the east.

"What do you think, Mr. Shilling?" Digano asked, pointing. "Your son's."

They walked up to the silent fighters. This was Robert's first point-blank look at Les's F-18, so close that he could read the block letters stenciled on the fuselage below the port side of the cockpit.

LT LES SHILLING

Underneath was his callsign.

HULK

Robert also saw the three-digit modex numbers on the nose. *Two-four-three* designated the squadron, the same numbers used in radio communication. Then it hit him hard. Robert felt proud of his son. Real proud.

A red-shirted ordnance man stood on the side of Les's fighter checking the AIM-9 Sidewinder heat-seeking missile on the port wing tip. On the starboard wingtip dangled another AIM-9. Strapped to the starboard and port inboard wings were two AIM-7 Sparrow radar-guided missiles. A brown-shirted plane captain—white rag in hand—was busy cleaning the metal area just below the cockpit Plexiglas. Like the other F-18 pilots, Les insisted on a clean fighter. The large, dark navy-issue boots used by the crews would often leave behind marks on the gray, dull-finished wings. Because of this dull camouflage scheme, the fighters never seemed to look properly clean.

"This is our flight deck," the commander explained, his hand resting on the port fuselage of Les's fighter near the nose. "We call it the *roof*. As you can see, two F-18s are ready for the launch. Shortly, these two aircraft will be placed on an Alert Five, meaning they will be armed and fueled, ready to be launched in five minutes. The pilots now are receiving their final briefing. We are only 200 miles from the Japanese shore."

"The Hornet is a unique fighter. It's simple enough for one pilot to fly. It's extremely versatile, an all-around, middle-weight, multi-role performer, with reliability, survivability, and ease of maintenance high on the priority list. Her service life is approximately 6,000 hours."

Digano slapped the fuselage. "She's made of aluminum, titanium, steel, graphite/epoxy, and various other materials. Graphite/epoxy covers forty percent of the surface area—the fins and the rudders mostly—but accounts for only nine percent of her weight.

"Start-ups are relatively simple in the Hornet. The pilot climbs in and hits the battery-operated APU, the Auxiliary Power Unit. This switch sends high-pressure air to the turbine starter to start each engine. Once the engine is lit, the Airframe Mounted Auxiliary Drive takes over. The AMAD is driven by a power shaft, which is connected to a fuel pump, a hydraulic pump and a generator, which kicks the engine over. This procedure eliminates the need for deck crews and ground support equipment getting in the way. You might say it's all self-contained. Now, if you follow me to the nearest elevator, I'll show you the hangar deck below us."

Inside the hangar deck, Cameron and Robert were impressed. To Robert, it was hard to believe that *Midway* was the smallest carrier in the United States arsenal. It was like another world below the flight deck, comparable to a small city. Several Hornets were lined up tail to tail, with many of them in various stages of maintenance. Men in coveralls were working on engines, removing and installing drop tanks. A tow truck was moving one fighter into place opposite one wall. Two other men were directing the driver for a proper park.

Digano led Cameron and Robert towards one F-18 where a four-man crew were installing a new engine with the aid of a sturdy dolly. The three stood back fifteen feet and watched the crew perform in an organized, coherent manner.

"Are either of you familiar with the F404 turbofan engine?" Digano asked.

"Not me," Cameron said.

"Me neither," Robert replied. "I'm a retired mechanic, but even a turbofan is new to me. I think I have the general idea, though."

"The best way to explain it," Digano continued, "is to say that there are turbojets and the more recent turbofans. A turbojet is a jet engine that has a turbo-driven compressor drawing in air at the front intake and forcing the compressed air into the combustion chamber. Into this chamber, fuel is injected and ignited. Hot gases rush through and drive the turbine. Fuel consumption can be brutal. The turbofan, on the other hand, has a by-pass tube where some of the incoming air goes around the combustion chamber and is pushed by a turbine-operated fan that mixes the air with the exhaust gases from the combustion chamber. This fan increases the air flow of the gases without sacrificing fuel consumption."

Robert nodded, watching a nearby F-18 crew installing an engine, noticing how easy it was for the men to slide the engine into place. "Times have sure changed, sir. Popping an engine in nowadays looks like a piece of cake."

"With the F404, the accent is on reliability and simple maintenance, and not brute force. Accessories are not mounted on the engine but rather on the airframe. A crew of four can change an engine in approximately twenty-five minutes. 'Within the shadow of the aircraft' as we call it."

Robert shook his head in amazement. If only things were done in the same way during the war.

"The F404 has a dry thrust of 10,600 pounds and max afterburning thrust of 16,000 pounds, putting her in the same class as the J79, which powers the F-4 Phantom, the aircraft the Hornet was built to replace. The F404 is half the weight, two-thirds the length, and contains thirty percent fewer components than the J79. The F404 is fitted with seven modules for quick repair and maintenance, while suspended vertically. Engine removal is only necessary when a problem arises that needs immediate attention or when a module exceeds its life span."

Suddenly, something in Digano's headphones caught his attention, jerking his head to one side. "Yes, sir, right away," he said into the headset. He turned to the two vets. "Gentlemen, let's go. There's action on the roof."

MARY JANE

Ainsworth bent over the navigator at his desk, and asked, "How far to the coast?"

Captain Marshall set down his pencil and calipers and pointed to his Mercator map. "In forty-five minutes, we'll reach the enemy coast, right here," he said. "The tip of this peninsula in Ise Bay. We go right up the Bay and turn here, at this point, for Lake Biwa."

Marshall and Ainsworth exchanged glances. Both knew that a few miles west of Lake Biwa stood the ancient and beautiful city of Kyoto. *The target.*

Ainsworth smiled, moving away. He realized he had less than an hour to make his move. The turning point at the end of Ise Bay was the springboard. For several moments he had been eyeing Marshall's maps and log notes. He fully understood navigational information such as true coarse, drift correction, true heading, magnetic heading that eventually arrived at the all-important compass heading. He had been studying such data secretly for months.

USS MIDWAY

General Cameron, Robert Shilling, and Commander Digano fixed themselves behind the observation deck—called Vulture's Row—on the carrier's island, all watching the launch scene unfold.

At first, it seemed disorganized. But the opposite was the case. The engines of the two F-18s were running. Deckmen scurried about, then disappeared to the sides. Blast deflectors behind the fighters flipped up. The engine noise grew louder and louder, until the exhausts turned a bright white. Robert plugged his ears with his fingers. He had never heard such thunder in his life. It was enough to punch pains in his stomach. Then, his son's aircraft screamed the length of the deck, flaming exhausts heating the surface. It was an impressive sight seeing Les's fighter clear the deck in the blink of an eye and climb, nose up, into the morning sky. Robert had a great rear-view of the hellish orange-white flames shooting from the fighter. Seconds later, Tiger's fighter bolted off the deck in the same shrieking fashion.

"Wow," was all that Robert could whisper, glancing at Cameron and Digano. They had just witnessed an afterburner launch, known as a Zone Five.

"Gentlemen," Digano broke the spell. "Commander Prentice would like us on the bridge."

Thirteen

Gail got up from the bed and slipped her nightgown on. Yawning, she sat on the bed and used the remote to flick on the small color TV. Typhoon Matilda was the first thing on her mind. Was it closer? Was it building up steam? She thumbed the button for CNN.

She turned up the volume. A male reporter was giving a weather advisory. He covered the details of Matilda's location, intensity, the direction she was moving, and the precautions to be taken. The eye of Matilda was now 1,100 miles to the southeast, ripping through the central portion of the Caroline Islands. Winds were packing 120 miles per hour. Ponape Island had already received ten inches of rain in the last twenty-four hours.

These Pacific typhoons weren't new to Gail. She and Les had weathered out one before. Gail figured that if Matilda's path veered towards Guam, it would probably reach the island in three or four days, providing that it traveled at the usual typhoon speed of 350 to 400 miles a day. Gail was an organized person, like most nurses. Even though no typhoon warning or typhoon watch had been issued for Guam yet—these were usually not done until twenty-four to thirty-six hours ahead—she was already thinking of stockpiling emergency foods, first-aid equipment, flashlights, battery packs, and filling the car's tank up with gas.

Through the window, she saw the strong winds were making the palm trees in the back yard sway. *A sign of worse things to come?*

"The colonel is up now, gentlemen," the pretty Japanese nurse notified David Shilling and Ensign Walker.

The men thanked her and hurried into Mason's room.

Same as the day before, Mason was found in his wheelchair, this time facing the door. A nurse inside quickly left. David sat on the couch nearest him. Walker stood.

"Colonel Mason, do you remember me? I'm David Shilling. Toshika and I came to visit you yesterday."

Mason looked slowly around the room. "Where is Toshika?"

"She's not here, colonel."

"I want to see Toshika."

"Colonel, you told me yesterday that you did intelligence work for the 509th Composite Group during the Second World War."

Mason stared across the room. "They dropped the atomic bombs."

"I know, Colonel Mason. What about the third atomic mission to Kyoto?"

Mason closed his eyes. "The third mission?"

Walker's face hardened. "The *third* atomic mission?" he whispered to David.

"Yes," David answered.

"Who are you?" Mason asked Walker.

David ignored the remark, then said, "You remember, colonel. I told you yesterday that my father was the crew chief of the *Mary Jane*. Do you remember what you said after that?"

"I'm too old to remember."

"Please try, colonel. You told me that the *Mary Jane* was on an atomic mission in 1945. Her target was Kyoto. Do you remember saying that?"

"I don't remember you. I want to see Toshika."

David sighed. "Colonel, did you work for air force intelligence during the war?"

Mason rubbed his face into his left hand. "Leave me be. Leave me be. I want my breakfast," he said slowly.

"Listen, colonel," David said, voice rising. "What was the codename for the Kyoto mission?"

"I think he's falling asleep, Mr. Shilling."

David stood. "*Ah, shit.* Now what?"

Confused, Walker shook his head. "What's going on here?"

David put one hand in his pocket and with the other nudged Mason until he woke with a jump. "Colonel?"

Mason looked up. "What do you want?"

David squatted down until his eyes were level with Mason's. "Colonel, did you like working for Mitsubishi after the war? You remember that Toshika's father also worked for Mitsubishi, don't you?"

"Where's Toshika. I don't know you. Who are you? Leave me alone!"

Walker leaned towards David and asked, "Who's Toshika?"

"A lady friend of mine."

"Well, we're not getting anywhere with him, ourselves. Why not get her—Toshika—down here?"

Both hands in his pockets, David replied, "I think I just may do that, Ensign Walker."

USS MIDWAY

Commodore Prentice paced the bridge, a hot mug of coffee in his hand. In addition to the regular men in position at their equipment, he was joined by the communications officer, Lieutenant Commander Gary Cross, a skinny individual with a face much younger than his thirty years. Prentice turned and acknowledged Cameron, Digano, and Robert as they entered the room.

"It's show time, gentlemen," Prentice said. "Let's see if we can talk Captain Clayton down. The audio communication on the bridge will soon be patched into the Combat Information Center, once we have made contact with the *Mary Jane*. By the flick of a switch on the console in front of me, we can speak directly to the F-18 or Captain Clayton himself. You'd better be convincing because the target first showed on radar only one hundred miles off the Japanese coast."

"We'll try," Cameron said.

"That means no word came through from my son yet on the codename?" Robert asked.

"Nothing."

"COMMODORE?" It was a voice over the CIC console.

Prentice pressed a button. "YES."

"WE'RE IN RADIO CONTACT WITH HULK AND TIGER, SIR. THEY HAVE A VISUAL OF THE TARGET AND HAVE ESTABLISHED RADIO CONTACT."

"PATCH ME IN ON THE FIGHTER FREQUENCY."

"AYE, AYE, SIR. COMMAND NINE."

Prentice only had to press a button marked "9" and was in immediate contact with Les Shilling.

"ZULU TWO-FOUR-THREE, THIS IS SCOUT ONE. DO YOU READ?"

"ZULU TWO-FOUR-THREE TO SCOUT ONE. I READ YOU."

"WHAT DO YOU HAVE FOR US, HULK? OVER."

"WE'RE A THOUSAND YARDS BEHIND HER. RADIO CONTACT HAS BEEN MADE WITH HAWKEYE THREE-SIX. THAT'S ALL. OVER."

"UNTIL FURTHER NOTICE, THE BRIDGE WILL TAKE OVER THE RADIO CONTACT WITH HAWKEYE THREE-SIX. THAT'S ALL. OVER."

"ROGER THAT, SCOUT ONE."

Prentice tapped another button for the CIC. "STEDNER?"

"SIR?"

"PATCH ME IN TO THE SAME FREQUENCY AS HULK AND THE MARY JANE."

"AYE, SIR. COMMAND TEN."

Prentice gestured for Cameron and Shilling to move closer to the metal microphone on the console. "Do your stuff, guys," he said, stepping back. "The radio communication is probably being monitored by the Japanese, but there's nothing we can do about it."

Cameron and Robert took seats by the microphone.

In order to convince Clayton, Cameron realized he had to use Baker Two, which was the callsign for Iwo Jima, where he waited out the *Mary Jane*'s mission forty-five years ago. Baker Two was the base and Cameron's specific callsign was Dimples. "HAWKEYE THREE-SIX, THIS IS BAKER TWO. DO YOU READ?"

"I READ YOU, BAKER TWO."

Cameron recognized Clayton's Southern accent. "THIS IS DIMPLES ONE."

"GO AHEAD, DIMPLES ONE."

"TURN BACK, HAWKEYE THREE-SIX. MISSION IS AN ABORT. THE JAPS HAVE SURRENDERED. DO YOU READ?"

"GIVE ME THE CODENAME, DIMPLES ONE."

Cameron swallowed hard. "THERE HAS BEEN A MIX-UP IN COMMUNICATIONS. LISTEN CLOSELY, HAWKEYE THREE-SIX. THERE–"

"HOW DO I KNOW YOU ARE THE REAL DIMPLES ONE?"

"LISTEN, IAN. YOUR AIRCRAFT IS THE MARY JANE. YOUR NAME IS IAN CLAYTON. YOU'RE FROM GEORGIA. THE BOMBER IS NAMED AFTER YOUR GIRLFRIEND BACK HOME IN ATLANTA. REMEMBER, THE ONE YOU SAID WAS STACKED? YOU HAD HER IMAGE PAINTED ON THE NOSE JUST BEFORE THE MISSION AT HAND. I FLEW WITH YOU IN EUROPE. THE EIGHTH AIR FORCE. REMEMBER THE NIGHT WE GOT DRUNK AND DROVE THE TRACTOR BACK TO THE BASE BECAUSE WE MISSED THE LAST TRAIN OUT?"

"NICE TRY, WHOEVER THE HELL YOU ARE. NOW I GOT A QUESTION FOR YOU. HOW COULD YOU BE CALLING FROM BAKER TWO? THE RECEPTION IS PERFECT. NO TRANSMITTER CAN REACH THIS FAR FROM THERE."

Cameron slipped his hand over the microphone, and leaned to Robert. "*Geez*, he's got us there. We didn't have the technology back then."

"Never mind. Keep going," Robert advised his friend.

"TURN BACK, HAWKEYE THREE-SIX. YOU WILL BE MAKING A TERRIBLE MISTAKE."

"IS THAT SO? GO TO HELL, WHOEVER YOU ARE. IT'S NOT GOING TO WORK, BUSTER. OVER AND OUT."

Cameron grunted.

"Ah, at least you tried," Robert said.

Prentice pressed his console button. "ZULU TWO-FOUR-THREE, THIS IS SCOUT ONE. ARE YOU THERE?"

"I'M HERE, SCOUT ONE. OVER."

"HOW FAR TO THE COAST?"

"WE JUST PASSED IT."

Prentice sighed for all the room to hear. "STAY ON HIS TAIL, ZULU TWO-FOUR-THREE. OVER."

"ROGER, SCOUT ONE."

JAPAN

Les had an idea and it was probably crazy enough to work.

"HAWKEYE THREE-SIX, THIS IS ZULU TWO-FOUR-THREE."

"STAY OFF THE AIR! WHAT HAPPENED TO RADIO SILENCE?"

"WE'RE COMING UP CLOSE TO ESCORT YOU. YOU MAY NEED US. OVER."

"WHAT!"

Les knew they weren't being monitored by enemy radio operators, only modern-day friendly operators. However, they were 31,000 feet over Japan. The Japanese authorities could start asking questions. Flight paths were required in such instances. Worse, what if the *Mary Jane* slipped into 1945 again, alone over enemy territory?

Off starboard, Les saw three vapor trails a few thousand feet above him in the morning sky. He looked to his right. Tiger was fifty feet away. He waved his hand to catch Tiger's attention. He pointed to himself, to Tiger, then to the B-29. Tiger nodded. *He got it.*

Les touched the throttles with his left hand. The rear view of *Mary Jane* came closer in seconds. He could almost reach out and touch the polished metal. Over the radio, he heard Commodore Prentice. "SCOUT ONE TO ZULU TWO-FOUR-THREE, DO YOU READ? SCOUT ONE—"

Then the transmission stopped cold. At the same time, Les felt a bang against his fighter, like a sudden wind turbulence. He looked up, twenty feet away, and saw the B-29's tail gunner, a camera up to his face, snapping pictures of the F-18. Off to the side, tucked in close, was Tiger and his own F-18

USS MIDWAY

"SIR, IT'S STEDNER."

Prentice hit the CIC button. "GO AHEAD."

"THEY'RE GONE OFF RADAR."

"GONE? WHAT DO YOU MEAN BY GONE?"

"HULK, TIGER AND THE MARY JANE WERE ON OUR SCOPE ONE SECOND AND THE NEXT SECOND THEY VANISHED. THAT'S WHAT I MEAN, SIR."

Prentice turned to scan the faces in the room. "They didn't. Tell me they didn't do it."

No one answered.

"THANKS, STEDNER. KEEP ME POSTED."

"AYE, AYE, SIR."

Prentice squeezed his forehead with his hand, as if he had a migraine. "I don't believe this. They're all back in 1945. They must be."

"And I know how they did it," Cameron said. "They all crowded in the same air space and when the *Mary Jane* went back to their own time, so did Tiger and Hulk. It sounds to me as if they planned it. Tiger and Hulk going back through time, I mean."

"Why?" Robert asked. "Why would they do it?"

"Defend the *Mary Jane*. Think of the possibilities. An F-18 can track and eliminate multiple targets. Two F-18s would be a terror over the skies of 1945 Japan. I kind of wish I was there," he smirked.

"But what if they don't come back?" Robert said, with feeling.

"As long as they stay close to the *Mary Jane*, they'll be back," Prentice assured Les's father as best he could.

"Let's consider something else here," the general said. "So far, we are all worried about the *Mary Jane* dropping this plutonium bomb in the present day. What if–"

"She drops it in 1945," Prentice finished off the sentence for Cameron.

"Exactly, commander."

"But it didn't go off in 1945. We know that from history."

"I know, commander. But history, here, now—for some reason—is not finished. Clayton *could* very well drop Fat Baby in 1945. Or enemy fighters may attack it. In that case, it was a smart move for Tiger and Hulk to go back to 1945 with the *Mary Jane*."

"Maybe it was," Prentice admitted. "I hope."

"Also," Cameron continued, "it might be a damn good idea to let Hulk and Tiger know, the next time we get them on the air, about the possibility of Fat Baby exploding in 1945. The fighter boys may be forced to shoot the *Mary Jane* down in 1945."

"Wait a minute," Robert said, his voice rising, "that means my son wouldn't make it back to the present."

Prentice waved his arms. "Let's not go crazy here. Nobody's going to shoot anything down in 1945. Let's just wait this out. Somebody go get us some coffee. Strong coffee!"

JAPAN

Les saw that the vapor trails he had seen earlier were gone. He glanced over his shoulder at Tiger in his F-18. They thumbed each other. Les then punched through the radio frequencies one at a time and was not surprised to hear a Japanese-language controller on one of the channels. Was he alerting fighters? Les had to think differently now. The Japanese were the enemy. *Remember Pearl Harbor.* He, Tiger, and the *Mary Jane* were all now in 1945. Son of a bitch, it worked.

Les shot a look over his wing and recognized Ise Bay from his 1990 days while stationed in Japan. Unmistakable shape to it. Kyoto was coming up. *The target.* He pressed the proper buttons on the right DDI to bring up the Track While Scan mode to search for enemy fighters. He selected a twenty-mile range and watched the screen. Then he changed back to the radio fighter frequency.

"ZULU TWO-FOUR-FOUR."

Tiger answered with a quick, "ROGER."

"DO YOU KNOW WHERE WE ARE, TIGER?"

"I'M WITH YUH. BUT I DON'T BELIEVE IT."

"STAY CLOSE. KEEP AN EYE ON YOUR RADAR. TWENTY-MILE RANGE. ANYTHING IS TO BE TREATED AS HOSTILE."

"ROGER."

Suddenly, a large, single blip appeared on Les's screen. More than ten miles. No visual. By its shape and size, he guessed it meant that several Japanese fighters were flying in close formation and showing up as one.

"I THINK WE GOT A BUNCHER, HULK."

"MY GUESS, TOO. LET'S SEPARATE 'EM."

"ROGER."

Les switched to the Raid Assessment mode. It was all laid out for him. His airborne Doppler beam radar separated four individual targets. According to the system, the targets were now splitting up into battle formation pairs at ten miles out and coming head on, twelve o'clock, still unseen by the naked eye.

This was too easy, Les thought. Air chivalry was a myth and he knew it. Air combat always and always will be an *I'll get you before you get me* approach, with the spoils going to the one who destroys the enemy before he himself is often even seen. The bravest or the strongest don't necessarily win. Just the smartest.

"ZULU TWO-FOUR-THREE TO ZULU TWO-FOUR-FOUR. THE TWO ON THE RIGHT ARE YOURS."

"ROGER. EASY MEAT."

Les let the Fly-by-Wire computer kick in. He no longer had to control the actual flight of the Hornet using stick and rudders. The FBW allowed Les to be free of any distractions and to concentrate on the targets. With one touch of his thumb on the stick, he adjusted the weapon select switch down. Two AIM-7 Sparrow missiles were ready for launching. The right DDI and HUD now displayed the Sparrow mode. The computer sorted through the targets. Les only had to pick and choose. *Two left*. With the stick, he lined up the pointer on the left radar dots one at a time. He had lock-on. With his forefinger, he fired the first radar-guided missile.

"FOX ONE," he announced to Tiger, signifying that a radar-guided Sparrow was launched. Then the second missile. *Fox Two.* In his headphones, he heard Tiger give the verbal signals for his own launches.

MARY JANE

Paul Lunsford, in his bombardier nose position, saw four fiery trails speeding towards a line of clouds.

"WHAT THE HELL WAS THAT?" he screamed into the intercom. "COMMANDER, DID YOU SEE THAT?"

"I SAW IT!"

"WHAT ARE THEY?"

"ROCKETS. I DON'T KNOW."

"WAIT, THERE'S FOUR BOGIES. SPREAD OUT. TWELVE O'CLOCK. LOOKIT THOSE ROCKETS MOVE!"

In seconds, all four targets exploded, one after another, the burning debris plummeting towards the water of Ise Bay.

Inside the cockpit, Clayton and Loran exchanged shocked stares, too stunned to speak. Lunsford did that for them.

"DID YOU SEE THAT! SON-OF-A-BITCH! OUR LITTLE FRIENDS DIDN'T HAVE TO MOVE. THEY FIRED THOSE ROCKETS AND SHOT DOWN FOUR BOGIES. HELL, I'M GLAD THESE GUYS ARE ON MY SIDE."

Ainsworth saw Les's F-18 through the navigator's window. He was confused. Fighters weren't supposed to escort *Mary Jane* over Japan. This wasn't part of the mission. They were getting in the way. Who were these fellahs with the twin-engined fighter planes with no props and weaponry so advanced that they could knock aircraft out of the sky before the pilots could even see them?

"NAVIGATOR TO COMMANDER."

Ainsworth turned to Dwight Marshall, who had called up Clayton on the intercom.

"I HEAR YOU, NAVIGATOR."

"ALTER COURSE TO THREE-ONE-ONE ON MY SIGNAL, COMMANDER."

This was Ainsworth's cue. *The turning point at Ise Bay.* Never mind the fighters. He nervously felt for his pistol beneath his Mae West and flight gear and took a few steps towards the cockpit, only a few feet away. He stopped directly behind Clayton just as Marshall gave the signal for the turning point at the very end of Ise Bay.

"IT'S COMING. HOLD ON. HERE WE ARE. ALTER COURSE TO THREE-ONE-ONE, COMMANDER."

"TURNING THREE-ONE-ONE."

Before Clayton could bank the Mary Jane to port, Ainsworth yanked the gun from beneath his flight gear and shoved the barrel against the back of Clayton's neck. The commander tried to pivot his head and look behind him, but Ainsworth pressed the barrel harder.

"Don't turn around!"

"Ainsworth, what yuh doing?"

"Shut up, and listen to me." Ainsworth stepped back so that he could see Loran, Clayton, and the others in the next compartment through the bulkhead opening. "Forget that heading, commander."

"Why?"

"We're not going to Kyoto. You have a new compass heading. Three-three-six."

"I hope this is a joke."

"It's no joke. Start turning to three-three-six. NOW!" Ainsworth stuck the gun even deeper into Clayton's skin.

"Take it easy!"

"Turn!"

The commander banked the bomber onto the new heading and leveled off, then asked, "Where we going?"

Ainsworth grinned. "Vladivostok," he replied, hoarsely. "That's in the Soviet Union, in case you don't know."

"That's at least six hundred miles away!"

"Three hours and we'll be there."

Clayton grunted. "You're a Russian agent, aren't you. I suppose your real name isn't Ainsworth?"

"That's right. I am Russian," Ainsworth replied with a Russian accent for the first time. "My real name is of no concern to you. Just fly. My country wants this bomb."

"Why?"

"*Why?* Are you crazy? We can rule the world with it."

Clayton glanced over at Loran. Both seemed calm.

"One bomb can't rule the world, Ainsworth. We've got more."

"No, you don't, commander. I know the Manhattan Project inside and out. I infiltrated it, along with a few others. You Americans won't have another atomic bomb ready for at least six months, maybe a year."

"What if we refuse to fly this bird to Russia?"

"I can fly it myself. I can easily deal with both of you and take this ship and fly it to the Soviet Union." Ainsworth glanced over his shoulder. Neither Emerson, Marshall, or Brown had made a move.

"Then why don't you?" Clayton said. "I don't think you've ever flown in your life."

"Shut up! Any wrong move and you get it in the back of the head."

"OK, OK." Clayton could see it would be wiser to keep things as calm as possible. "How are we expected to land with a fully armed atomic bomb aboard? It could go off and kill us all. Then you wouldn't have anything, pal."

"I know what you're trying to do, dammit. You. . . you think you can try something when I'm back in the bomb bay disarming Fat Baby. Well, I got news for you. I still have the red plugs. I never did replace the green ones. She's not armed."

Clayton knew he had to keep Ainsworth talking. "What about those two fighters following us? Once we're over the Sea of Japan, they might take some action."

"Who says they will?"

Clayton had to agree. What to do now? He was beginning to believe that Ainsworth—or whatever his name was—was acting on his own. A Russian conspiracy couldn't be behind such a kooky plan. Ainsworth had to be nuts!

KYOTO

"Toshika, am I glad to see you."

David and Walker met Toshika in the front lobby.

"This is Ensign Walker."

"Pleased to meet you, ma'am," Walker said, cordially.

"Ensign," Toshika replied. "What's this all about, you two?" she asked, red-faced, visibly annoyed. "I came as soon as I could. I'm afraid it wasn't easy getting away. The traffic is horrible." She shot a stare at David. "Why couldn't you tell me over the phone?"

"Security, ma'am," Walker said.

David put his hand on her shoulder. "I wouldn't have asked you here if it wasn't important. Believe me. We need you to speak to the colonel for us. He has some information we need. Besides, he keeps asking for you."

She seemed to relax. "What information?"

"He knows the codename for the Kyoto atomic mission."

"This again? I told you, David, don't listen to the colonel."

David took a breath to control his sudden anger. "There *were* three missions. This has been confirmed. OK. *Confirmed.* My father's bomber, the *Mary Jane*, really did carry an atomic bomb. I have been ordered by the US Navy to find the codename for the mission. I don't know why, but it must be found. They need it and I need your help because I can't get through to the colonel."

"I see," Toshika replied, after a long silence. "OK, let's go. But I have to warn you. Today could be one of those bad days."

Fourteen

It was a single projectile
Charged with all the power of the universe.
An incandescent column of smoke and flame
As bright as ten thousand suns
Rose in all its splendor. . .
It was an unknown weapon,
An iron thunderbolt,
A gigantic messenger of death
Which reduced to ashes
The entire race of the Vrishnis and the Andhakras
. . .The corpses were so burned
As to be unrecognizable.
Their hair and nails fell out;
Pottery broke without cause,
And the birds turned white.

the ancient Sanskrit writings of Mahabharata

JAPAN
"ZULU TWO-FOUR-THREE, THIS IS A WIDE BOMB RUN. MARY JANE IS OFF COURSE."

Les looked down at the northern coast of Japan. The white caps of the Sea of Japan blinked ahead. Tiger was right. Clayton was drifting off course, unless he was going to take a wide bank over the water and head south to the target. But that would leave the bomber over enemy territory for too long.

125

"LET'S JUST STAY WITH HIM, TIGER."

"ROGER."

Suddenly, tracers flew by, barely missing the F-18s. Les glanced behind. Two prop-driven fighters—Zeros for sure—were bearing down. More tracers, then the Zeros shot past, directly underneath. There didn't seem to be any hits. The Zeros banked to the far left and began to turn to starboard more than two miles out.

"LOOKS LIKE ANOTHER ATTACK COMING UP ON OUR SIX, TIGER."

"YEAH. LET ME TAKE A CRACK AT 'EM."

Les considered the request. They just couldn't hang underneath the *Mary Jane* and hope that no Jap ammo found its mark. If either he or Tiger, or the *Mary Jane* for that matter, were shot down, no one would return intact to 1990. They had no choice.

"GO BOUNCE 'EM, TIGER. MAKE IT QUICK AND GET BACK HERE."

"ROGER."

Tiger eased away from the bomber, shoving the throttles forward.

Les watched and changed frequencies. "ZULU TWO-FOUR-THREE TO HAWKEYE THREE-SIX. ZULU TWO-FOUR-THREE TO HAWKEYE THREE SIX."

"I HEAR YUH, LITTLE FRIEND."

"DON'T MOVE. THE ZEROS WON'T BOTHER YOU ANYMORE. THEY'RE DEAD MEAT."

"SAY AGAIN. DEAD WHAT?"

"NEVER MIND. JUST STAY WHERE YOU ARE."

Watching the Zeros banking, Tiger cut in front of their intended path by several thousand yards and pulled the stick towards him. The F-18 climbed into the sky, almost straight up. After 3,000 feet in a vertical climb, he whipped the fighter over and came in 2,000 yards behind the Zeros. The Zeros—making a run for it—banked off in opposite directions. He then raced between them at a speed of more than Mach 1. He banked to port and felt the G-forces build against his body. He tensed his stomach and leg muscles. The G-line on the HUD climbed to 6-G before he leveled the fighter and came up again from behind, this time at less than 500 yards. The two fighters were forming up again, only thirty yards apart. He throttled back to give them some lead.

Tiger flicked a button on the column to call up the Air Combat Maneuvering mode, in particular the Boresight mode. He pointed the nose at the left Zero. The HUD displayed a twenty-degree horizontal and vertical search and locked up the targets one at a time. He pressed the weapons select switch on the column to the down position. *Sidewinder mode. Two heat-seeking missiles waiting.* The noses of the Sidewinders were so sensitive to any type of heat that they would relay a constant rattle into the pilot's headphones once he lined onto another aircraft. Tiger heard the rattle. He squeezed the trigger on the stick. Two heat-seeking missiles on their way.

He banked severely to starboard.

Inside the *Mary Jane*, most of the crew, including Clayton and Loran, saw the two bright explosions.

Ainsworth stood amazed. "That's incredible!"

It was Clayton's chance. He grabbed the controls and yanked them hard to the left, then to the right. Ainsworth, the only one not strapped in, flew across the cockpit. His head banged against the back of Clayton's seat, but he still managed to hold onto the pistol. Loran unstrapped himself and jumped at Ainsworth, punching him hard on the mouth. They struggled for the gun, four sweaty hands in death lock. The two rolled over and over.

"Come on, Four Eyes, give it up!" Loran screamed while on his back, Ainsworth on top of him.

Before they knew it, two shots fired upwards into the fuselage.

"Watch it!" Clayton shouted over his shoulder. "Butch, get in there!"

Butch Emerson joined in to help, but two more shots exploded. Emerson was able to grab the gun and with Ainsworth holding it, and pointed the barrel into Ainsworth stomach. Emerson pulled the trigger.

Twice.

Ainsworth slumped on his back to the deck, his stomach bleeding. Emerson struggled to his knees and fired the pistol once more directly into Ainsworth's chest.

"Bastard!"

"Easy, Butch, he's dead." Loran took the gun from Emerson. "Thanks."

Smoke and the smell of cordite filled the air. The cockpit began to cool off quickly.

"We're losing cabin pressure!" Clayton cried out. "Paul!" He pointed upwards with one hand, hanging onto the wheel with the other. "Plug up the holes!"

Lunsford grabbed some clean rags he had kept at his station and jumped into the cockpit.

"COMMANDER TO NAVIGATOR. I NEED A COURSE TO LAKE BIWA."

"GIVE ME A SECOND, SIR."

Lunsford saw two holes a few inches apart above the commander's head. He ripped one of the rags into two pieces and rolled up one section. In thirty seconds, he had both holes plugged firmly. "There," he said.

"I can still feel cold air," Clayton said. "And it's getting harder to breath."

Loran agreed. He got down on his knees and checked each side of the fuselage. "There—to the right of my seat. Two holes." He could see that the bullets had just missed the intercom jack box by inches.

Ripping another piece of rag in half, Lunsford handed one piece to Loran, who shoved it in place. The temperature began to rise and breathing became easier.

"That's more like it," Clayton said. "Thanks, guys." He saw Emerson searching through Ainsworth's pockets. "Butch, what are you doing?"

"Trying to find the red plugs, sir. Here they are," he said, holding them in his hand. "All three of them." He showed them to his skipper. "I guess I'll be the one to put the little buggers in."

"Get ready," Clayton encouraged him. "But wait, the bomb bay is unheated and unpressurized. You'll have to release the pressure in our compartment so that you can open the hatch. We have no choice but to insert the red plugs at high altitude because we can't afford to drop down 20,000 feet. The Japs will swarm all over us."

"I understand, sir."

"Hurry, damn it!"

"I'm going."

"NAVIGATOR TO COMMANDER. I GOT THE FIRST TURNING POINT FOR YOU."

Through light cloud, Tiger saw Les and the *Mary Jane* at three o'clock, three or four miles off. They had changed direction and were back on the bomb run. He pushed forward on the throttles to catch up, banking slightly a few degrees to starboard.

"ZULU TWO-FOUR-THREE, THIS IS ZULU TWO-FOUR-FOUR. TARGETS DESTROYED.

"ROGER, ZULU TWO-FOUR-FOUR. I HAVE A VISUAL OF YOU."

Tiger was only three hundred yards off now. Then. . . the bomber and Hulk both disappeared.

KYOTO

Toshika stood beside the wheelchair and shook the sleeping Mason by the shoulders. "Colonel."

Mason opened his eyes, looking up at her. "Toshika, is that you?"

"Yes, it is, colonel." She found a chair, smiled, and sat awkwardly. "Did you enjoy your breakfast?"

"No, it was terrible."

Toshika grinned. "Come now, it couldn't have been that bad."

"It was so!"

Toshika knew it was no use arguing with him. "Colonel, is it true you were an officer in the United States Air Force during World War II?"

"Yes. . . it is true. I was in S-2."

"S-2?" Toshika whispered to David in his direction.

"Intelligence section, ma'am," Walker said.

"Intelligence, is that right, colonel?"

The colonel nodded at Toshika's next question. She reached out and held his hand. "Colonel, was there really a third atomic mission called on our country? I want the truth."

It took Mason a long time before he responded. Finally, he said, "It's top secret. I promised President Truman that I would never tell anybody who didn't need to know."

"But you told David and me yesterday."

Surprised, he answered, "Did I?"

"Yes, you did. David's father knew the crew of the *Mary Jane*, the bomber that you said had left its base to bomb Kyoto with a plutonium bomb."

Mason stared off, glassy-eyed. "Something went wrong."

"What went wrong?"

"I can't tell you. I promised President Truman."

"Truman's been dead for years. You don't owe him anything. What was the codename, colonel?"

"I can't do it."

"Do you remember it?"

"Yes, I do. With that codename I had power. The entire Army Air Force was at my beck and call. A mere mention of the name could cancel the mission, even make the *Mary Jane* turn around in mid-flight."

"Please tell us the codename, colonel," Toshika pleaded. "The US Navy needs it. Nothing will happen to you, honest."

David stepped forward, red-faced. "OK, that's it. Colonel, let's finish this thing right here. I'm sure the US Navy doesn't want to waste anyone's time. This isn't a game. The navy pulled me out of bed at five this morning to get the codename from you. Now tell us the damn codename. Now!"

"David, please," Toshika said. "Colonel, listen to me. We're not leaving until we get the codename. So tell us. Truman won't roll over in his grave. He'd understand. We want it!"

The colonel folded his hands in his lap. Tears began to form in his eyes. He looked around the room. Then his lips quivered. Finally. . . he uttered. . . a breathy, "Electron."

Mary Jane

"COMMANDER TO CREW IN THE FORWARD COMPARTMENT. WE ARE ON A NEW COURSE TO LAKE BIWA. GRAB YOUR FLYING SUITS AND AN OXYGEN PACK. IT'S GOING TO GET COLD IN HERE IN A FEW MINUTES. GO!"

Emerson fitted his hands into a pair of thin, silk navigator gloves he had borrowed from Dwight Marshall. He shrugged on his flight jacket and strapped on his portable oxygen cylinder. He checked the pressure gauge, which read a healthy 450 pounds per square inch. The cylinder contained six to twelve minutes of oxygen, depending on the amount of activity. Then he bent under his flight engineer's seat where the cabin pressure relief valve was located. He turned the valve slowly. This procedure was necessary to prevent the inside pressure rupturing the fuselage skin, as well as preventing loose material being sucked towards the bomb bay hatch.

Clayton reached for his thick leather jacket and oxygen mask. "COMMANDER TO FORWARD CREW. GIVE ME A CALL-IN WHEN YOU'RE READY. NOSE TO TAIL. LET'S GO."

Lunsford waved from the nose, jacket and mask already in place. "BOMBARDIER HERE. I'M READY."

Loran nodded, thumbs up.

"NAVIGATOR OK."

"RADIO A-OK."

Clayton turned to Emerson, flashlight in hand, who looked all set as he too gave the thumbs up. Emerson opened the hatch and climbed in the bomb bay. Immediately, he could feel the bitter cold air hit the exposed skin on his face. *Shit, it was freezing.* At this altitude of 31,000 feet, the temperature had to be in the fifty-below range. Carefully and methodically, he turned each of the three green plugs counterclockwise until they popped off. Then, one at a time, he injected the first two red plugs. With cold hands, he reached into his jacket for the third and final plug.

"There you are," he muttered to the third plug. But before he could screw it into place, he dropped it. *Shit!* Frantic, he ran the flashlight along the bottom of the bomb bay. "Clayton will kill me if I don't find it," he said to himself.

He searched and searched. . . then found it. . . under the nose of the bomb. "Thank God," he whispered, picking the plug up. "Come to papa." He checked his oxygen pack. Only three minutes left.

In the cockpit, Clayton was getting nervous. What was taking Emerson so long? He saw a large, long lake through the glass. Out the side, one of the crazy fighters was still with him. Where was the other?

"NAVIGATOR TO COMMANDER. TURN FIVE DEGREES LEFT. TWO MINUTES TO LAKE BIWA."

"ROGER. TURNING FIVE LEFT."

On the navigator's orders, Clayton banked slightly to the left. Five degrees. It was quickly becoming cold in the cockpit. He hadn't worn an oxygen mask and flight jacket in more than a year, since his days with the Eighth Air Force in Britain. The rubber against his skin felt too tight. But only a few minutes more. *Where the hell was Emerson?*

"NAVIGATOR TO COMMANDER. TURN TWO-TWO-SIX."

Clayton felt a tap on his shoulder. He turned to see Emerson giving the OK sign with his thumb, under the silk navigator glove. Fat Baby was armed for good.

Clayton smiled under his oxygen mask. "COMMANDER TO NAVIGATOR, TURNING TWO-TWO-SIX."

USS MIDWAY

"ZULU TWO-FOUR-THREE, THIS IS SCOUT ONE. DO YOU READ?" Commodore Prentice said, hoping to catch up with Les Shilling. Where were they? "ZULU TWO-FOUR-THREE, THIS IS SCOUT ONE. DO YOU READ?"

The answer finally came. "ROGER, SCOUT ONE. ZULU TWO-FOUR-THREE READING YOU. OVER."

"THANK GOD YOU'RE BACK WITH US. WHAT'S YOUR PRESENT POSITION?"

"JUST PASSED NORTHERN EDGE OF LAKE BIWA. LINING UP FOR IP RUN. WE WENT OFF COURSE AND LOST SOME MINUTES. ANY NEWS FROM KYOTO?"

"NEGATIVE. HOW WAS THE TRIP?"

"SIX BOGIES TO ONE OF OURS. OVER."

"YOU MEAN TIGER BOUGHT IT?"

"NEGATIVE. LOST IN TIME, IF YOU KNOW WHAT I MEAN."

"AFFIRMATIVE. I GET THE PICTURE. WE'LL KEEP IN TOUCH. SCOUT ONE OUT."

Prentice spun around to face the others in the room. Tiger lost? They looked as astonished as Prentice.

JAPAN

Tiger searched the skies for several minutes over Lake Biwa.

No Mary Jane.

No Hulk.

No high vapor trails.

This was it. He was stuck in 1945.

He checked his fuel. Down to one-third of his take-off load. The drop tanks were gone. Maybe 500 to 600 miles left, if he was lucky and conserved his fuel. One option was to fly to the Soviet Union. They were supposed to be allies during the war. What would they do with him? Probably keep his oddball fighter and, if he was fortunate, he might be sent back to the States after months of internment. From the stories he had heard, he knew it was more likely that starvation or execution faced him in a Soviet jail. *Some ally.*

No, Tiger was going down a hero. And have some fun.

She was nearing the far end of Lake Biwa, twenty-five miles—eight minutes—from the IP. The cabin temperature was back to a normal seventy degrees inside the forward compartment. Oxygen masks, electrically-heated suits, flight jackets, gloves were all discarded.

Clayton glanced over at Loran. They nodded at each other.

They flew on, the engines droning.

"IP COMING UP IN TWO MINUTES, COMMANDER. ALTER COURSE TWO-SIX-FIVE ON MY SIGNAL."

"ROGER."

Clayton saw scattered cloud to the west of the lake, the direction of the target. He needed at most three-tenths cloud to bomb the target.

One more minute. . .

The strange fighter still stuck close by, Clayton picking out the needle nose through the port side of the Plexiglas. He checked his watch. The mission was fifteen minutes overdue. *Damn that Four Eyes.* Clayton looked down. He saw boats on the lake, six miles below. Ahead, off port, the peninsula—the IP—jutted into the water.

In the tail, Gabriel Schwartz kept his eyes open for enemy aircraft. *None.* But he did think it strange that some contrails were *above* them. They had to be 40,000 feet. Could Zeros fly that high? In the radar room, Mark Crosby didn't see anything out of the ordinary on his equipment, except for Lake Biwa below. There was no mistake about that. Nevin Brown was catching some crazy songs on his radio set. At the flight engineer's position, Emerson studied his panel. There seemed to be enough fuel left to make Tinian.

Dwight Marshall glanced out his navigator's window. He recognized the Lake Biwa peninsula, which was the spot where a number of shrines stood. "NAVIGATOR TO COMMANDER, IN TEN SECONDS OUR NEW COMPASS HEADING SHOULD BE TWO-SIX-FIVE."

Lunsford peered into the Norden bomb sight. Dead ahead—Otsu City, the community that bordered Lake Biwa. He then recalled the aerial photos he had studied on the ground prior to the mission. Otsu City was spread out and had more buildings than he had remembered from the snapshots. *Had it grown that much?* But it had to be Kyoto ahead because beyond Otsu he saw the hills that separated the port city from Kyoto. Everything checked out.

133

In the cockpit, Loran closed his eyes for a moment and said a quick, silent prayer to his maker that all would go well.

"THIS IS IT, COMMANDER. TURN TWO-SIX-FIVE."

"ROGER. TURNING TWO-SIX-FIVE," Clayton answered his navigator. He banked ever so slightly to starboard. They were now on their initial point. Six miles, two minutes to go. "COMMANDER TO CREW. PUT ON YOUR SAFETY GLASSES."

The crew obeyed, most of them adjusting the glasses so that they were blacked out completely. Loran, Clayton, and Lunsford left their glasses on their foreheads because they couldn't perform their work otherwise.

"COMMANDER TO BOMBARDIER. OPEN BOMB BAY."

"ROGER." Lunsford slid his left hand down to a panel on his left and hit the toggle switch. He heard and felt the vibrations when the mighty bomb bay doors creaked open.

This is where I get lost, Les thought. He wasn't going to stick around for the lethal explosion. He gave port rudder and stick, soaring away from the *Mary Jane.*

Unless the bomber was stopped, his brother would die in the blast. Tears came to Les's eyes. If he wanted, he could have blown the *Mary Jane* out of the sky at a safe distance of thirty miles. All on radar. No visual. But that would mean shooting the B-29 down without authorization. Despite the predicament, Les's loyalty was to his country and the US Navy.

And that's what hurt.

USS MIDWAY

Lieutenant Commander Cross, the communications officer, buzzed the bridge.

"COMMODORE?"

"COMMODORE PRENTICE HERE."

"SIR, IT'S CROSS. THE CODENAME JUST CAME THROUGH FROM YOKO-SUKA."

"WELL, WHAT IS IT?"

"ELECTRON."

"THANKS, COMMANDER. GOOD WORK. OUT."

Prentice glared at Cameron. "You're on, general."

134

MARY JANE

In the viewfinder, Lunsford could see the eastern suburbs of Kyoto through a large gap in the clouds. He was astonished how clear it was. Cars, roads, rooftops, greenery. It was Kyoto, all right. The joining of the Kamo and the Takano rivers was unmistakable. A mile southwest stood the historical Imperial Gardens. The apex of the rivers was drifting into the bombsight's cross hairs.

"COMMANDER TO CREW. ARE WE IN AGREEMENT THIS IS KYOTO?"

Lunsford answered first. "IT'S KYOTO, COMMANDER."

The other crew members followed in the same identification.

The cross hairs were slowly lining up on the joint of the rivers. Lunsford made his final adjustments on the bomb sight. *Seconds away now.* He was just about to hit the tone signal that would give off a constant hum for the final seconds of the bomb run. . . when the commander hit the intercom.

"HOLD ON, PAUL."

"WHAT! I GOT HER LINED UP!"

"HOLD ON, I SAID!"

USS MIDWAY

Seated beside the bridge console, Cameron repeated the message.

"HAWKEYE THREE-SIX, THIS IS DIMPLES ONE. ABORT MISSION. ELECTRON! REPEAT, ELECTRON! DO YOU READ, HAWKEYE THREE-SIX."

MARY JANE

"He gave the codename, Ian. What do we do?" Loran said, excited.

Clayton shrugged. "We have no choice but to turn back."

"After all we've been through, they're going to cancel the mission! The city's in our bombsight! Something's fishy."

"Maybe the Japs did surrender like Dimples One said."

"HAWKEYE THREE-SIX, THIS IS DIMPLES ONE. PLEASE ACKNOWLEDGE LAST MESSAGE. OVER."

Clayton pressed the radio button. "I HEARD YUH, DIMPLES ONE. WE'RE TURNING AROUND."

Loran shook his head. "I don't get it."

"COMMANDER TO CREW. MISSION IS AN ABORT. REPEAT MISSION IS AN ABORT. CLOSE UP THE BOMB BAY, PAUL. WE'RE PACKING UP AND

HEADING HOME." He turned to Loran. "Geez, Carl, what a ride this has been!"

USS MIDWAY

The bridge cheered. Prentice shook hands with Cameron and Robert Shilling.

Robert was elated. His son was safe. Actually, both sons were safe.

Prentice buzzed the CIC. "STEDNER."

"YES, COMMANDER."

"LET HULK KNOW THE BOMBER'S RECEIVED THE CODENAME AND HAS TURNED OFF THE BOMB RUN."

"AYE, AYE, SIR. WITH PLEASURE!"

MacDonald was delighted and went around shaking hands and patting men on the back. "There, it's finally put to rest," he said to Cameron.

"Looks like it," Cameron replied. But he wasn't that convinced. He remembered the *Mary Jane* was found intact on Guam. How did that happen? Was something still missing? A scene left unplayed?

"What were Clayton's orders now?"

"Disarm the bomb and drop it in the ocean," Cameron answered MacDonald, the celebration around them.

"That means the crew will go back to their own time. And goodbye *Mary Jane*. We have Typhoon Matilda to worry about now. We had better get back to Guam."

We'll see if this is the end, Cameron thought. Suddenly, he realized that in 1945 dropping an A-bomb into the ocean wasn't a problem. But in 1990, with greater awareness of environmental hazards, an atomic bomb on the ocean floor could be a great risk. If Fat Baby was dropped in the Pacific, the salt water would dissolve the metal casing causing the plutonium to eventually leak out. If dropped in 1990, however, then at least the US Navy might have time to take appropriate action.

Should I say something?

This wouldn't be the first naval nuclear accident. He recalled an incident that had taken place twenty-five years earlier near the island of Okinawa, where a US Navy hydrogen-bomb-equipped A-4E Skyhawk strike aircraft had fallen off the flight deck of the carrier *Ticonderoga* and was never found. And what about the handful of nuclear Russian subs that were probably at the bottom of the Pacific and the Atlantic, including the one he had read about in *The Devil Seas*?

Oh, what to do.

"We're forgetting something," Cameron said out loud. The room grew quiet.

"What's that?" Prentice asked.

"We lost a fighter pilot today. Tiger is gone."

Prentice sighed. "That's right. Thanks for the jolt of reality, general. Lost in time. Imagine."

"Could we at least drink a toast to him?"

Fifteen

It didn't take Tiger long to find a Japanese military air base. From 25,000 feet up, he saw runways crisscrossing north of Osaka. He performed a series of wide, slowly descending circles over the base, at the same time keeping his eyes open for enemy fighters on patrol. He made one low pass over the tower at 1,000 feet to have a look and turned away to come around again. This time, he screamed across one runway at 100 feet, hurtling towards the hangars at a speed of 500 knots. Up and down the hardstands were closely-parked, single-engine fighters that he recognized as Zeros. Fifteen of them at a guess. He was close enough to see their camouflage colors. Several people near the planes scrambled for cover. To the left, one of the fighters had just touched down and was about to hang a left onto the taxi strip. Tiger banked to starboard so that he could meet the fighter head-on for the next pass.

For armament, Tiger was now down to the nose-mounted cannon, his four missiles used up. He flicked to GUN on the weapon-select switch. The HUD displayed the gun mode, complete with a reticle and gunfire impact point to aim for. The modern Hornet was full of wizardry, but Tiger wanted to operate the system manually, just like the good old strafing days of World War II.

By the time Tiger banked and came around again, the anti-aircraft fire had opened up on him. But the gunners couldn't find the range. Tiger was much too fast. At 400 knots, he brought the F-18 right down to the deck—100 feet—and held his finger on the trigger. Two lines of 20mm cannon firing 100 rounds a second chewed a path towards the fighter until she exploded into a fierce fireball. Tiger pulled his F-18 straight up, over the explosion, giving full throttle. He heard small pieces of debris banging against the underbelly. He quickly checked the instruments for any damage. *No change. Nothing.*

By now, more distant black puffs appeared in the sky, the closest explosion two or three hundred feet off his port wing. He outran the puffs as he poured on the afterburners and soared into the sky in a near-vertical climb. At 15,000, he looped the Hornet over and aimed for the base. Once again, he brought the fighter down to the deck, five hundred yards from the nearest target. Closing in, he aimed for the line of fighters on the dispersal track. He wanted as many as he could get in his final pass. Fifty yards away, at a height of eighty feet, he pressed the stick trigger and held it down until he passed the line of airplanes and he was out of ammo. All 570 rounds. He banked to port to look over his wing. Three fighters were in flames. Then a fourth exploded. Followed by a fifth. Suddenly, Tiger was rocked by a flak burst. The instruments to the port side told him the port engine was on fire. He quickly lit the extinguisher button to douse the flames. Then he shut down the engine, skimming the ground at 400 knots. His digital display told him he had a fuel leak. He turned the fighter away from Osaka, towards Osaka Bay, and brought the nose up until he reached 2,000 feet.

Now what?

Tiger was still finding it hard to believe where he actually was. He was stuck in August 1945, mere days before Japan surrendered. About three days. He could abort and send the fighter into the bay. Could he hide out for three days? What other choice did he have at the moment?

Osaka Bay loomed dead ahead, a distance of two or three miles. Tiger determined that 200 miles of fuel remained in the tanks, which meant that if the fighter kept to its present course, it would run out of fuel over the ocean. By now, half the Japanese air force were probably looking for him and his aircraft. He quickly made up his mind that no one would find the F-18.

Tiger glanced below. All the way out to the bay looked deserted, only a single road and a few odd buildings close together, others scattered. He flicked the stick-mounted autopilot on with his little finger. He disconnected the canopy and was immediately met by a stunning turbulence of air. He was ready for ejection.

The F-18 Hornet was fitted with the Navy Common Ejection Seat, which contained a fully automatic step-by-step system of escape, controlled by an electronic sequencer. Tiger engaged it by pulling a loop—the seat firing handle—situated between his thighs on the front part of the pilot seat. A rocket exploded below him, sending him through the top of the aircraft, seat and all, his leg restraints keeping his legs together. Once Tiger was free of the fighter, a rocket motor beneath the seat fired the drogue deployment catapult as it reached the end of its stroke. Then a parachute deployment rocket fired. His leg restraint system freed his legs, and his seat fell to earth. In a short time, his parachute inflated and he was descending slowly. He glanced southward, at the last sight of his fighter. Only the starboard engine was belching red.

Now came the tricky part, avoiding the authorities. *Was this really happening?*

GUAM

By mid-afternoon, the Super Stallion crew brought Robert Shilling, General Cameron, and Captain MacDonald back to Agana, Guam. When they stepped off the helicopter they could see for themselves that the winds had increased and the skies had grayed over.

"Matilda's getting closer," Cameron said, scanning the threatening skies.

Les was already at home by the time his father and Cameron had arrived by a US Navy staff car. Gail, Les, and Edna met them on the front steps.

"Where's Denise?" Cameron asked Gail about his wife.

She motioned towards the kitchen. "On the phone. A long-distance call came through from the States."

Flustered, Denise appeared in an instant.

"Denise, what's wrong?" Cameron asked her.

"It's my sister, Mary. She just had a heart attack and is in hospital in San Francisco."

"Will she pull through?"

"They think she will. But she may suffer some lasting effects. Phil, we have to see her on the way back."

"Of course," Cameron agreed. "But for now, we have to stay on Guam

141

with the Shillings until this typhoon blows through. I can't desert now. You know how it is."

Les wouldn't hear of it. "It's too dangerous to stay, General Cameron. There are flights leaving the island every day. The best thing is to get on the next one out of here."

"I can't leave, Les. I wouldn't feel right. You understand, dear," Cameron said, appealing to his wife. "Bob and I have talked it over. We are going to ship you and Edna somewhere safe and we'll come later. In fact, go on to San Francisco now."

Denise smiled, hugging her husband. "I understand."

"Sorry, Les," Robert said, taking Cameron's side, "we're here to stay. You'll need help. Somebody has to stick around. The whole island can't be vacated."

MARY JANE

Captain Clayton waved his flight engineer to come over to the cockpit.

"Yes, sir, captain."

"We're over a hundred miles from the coast and should be out of enemy fighter range shortly. Of course you realize what you have to do, do you?"

Emerson nodded. He knew, but he didn't like it. "I have to reverse the whole procedure and disarm the bomb completely." He looked down at his hands to the loading checklist he had retrieved from Ainsworth's pockets.

"Can you do it?"

"I don't know for sure. I'm no explosives expert. That was Ainsworth's field, not mine."

"How about the two of us figure it out together, OK?"

"OK, captain. I'd appreciate that."

In another twenty minutes, Clayton dropped the bomber down to 9,000 feet. Then he left the flying to Loran as he followed Emerson into the bomb bay.

Squatting at the front of the bomb, the two studied the checklist by the light of the flashlight. Emerson opened the toolbox.

"First off," Clayton said, "we've got to pull those red plugs out."

"Right."

"Then we have to disconnect the firing lines and the explosive charge. Right?"

"Seems so, captain."

"Let's go."

JAPAN

Two hundred feet from the ground, Tiger watched helplessly as what appeared to be a brown army truck drove along a road several miles to his left. Fortunately, it was moving away from him. *Had they not seen him?* Below was a forest, which was good. . . and bad. The forest would hide him for a time—perhaps for a long time—from his pursuers. But it also contained sharp branches that could spear through him during the descent. Off to the right, more than a mile, was an open field. Beyond that some buildings, surrounded by colorful gardens.

The trees were coming up fast. Tiger braced himself. He aimed for a slight opening between two trees.

He closed his eyes. He heard and felt a *thunk* that jolted his body. He had stopped. He couldn't feel the ground beneath him. He opened his eyes to find that he was hanging three feet from the ground, his parachute tangled to the top of a tree. What luck! All he had to do was loosen the parachute clip and jump to the ground. He looked up and pulled the parachute through the branches and left it lying there.

Taking a deep breath, he started running towards the open field.

MARY JANE

Clayton and Emerson climbed from the hatch. They were both sweating, but they had done it. The bomb was disarmed.

"What should we do with Ainsworth?" Emerson asked, closing the hatch door.

"I don't know. Drop him in the hatch and let him go out with the bomb. He's dead anyway. Get someone to give you a hand." Clayton returned to the cockpit pilot seat.

A short time later, Emerson tapped Clayton on the shoulder. "He's in, captain."

"All right, Paul, open it up!" he yelled to the bombardier.

"You bet, sir."

For a second time that day, Lunsford hit the bomb bay toggle switch and again he heard the vibrations of the bomb bay doors opening.

In the tail, Gabriel Schwartz saw Ainsworth's body fall clear, along with the bomb. *Geez, Fat Baby was huge,* he thought.

"COMMANDER TO TAIL GUNNER. WHAT DO YOU SEE?"

"THE BOMB AND AINSWORTH ARE BOTH OUT, SIR. YOU CAN CLOSE UP THE BOMB BAY."

Schwartz continued to watch. He saw the bomb splash the water, followed by Ainsworth's body. Schwartz pressed his intercom button. "TAIL TO COMMANDER. FAT BABY JUST HIT THE WATER AND MADE ONE GOOD SIZE SPLASH. I SEE AINSWORTH'S BODY FLOATING."

Dwight Marshall quickly made a longitude and latitude notation in his log on where the bomb had been jettisoned.

Clayton wiped his face with the back of his hand and smiled at Loran. "THANKS, TAIL. COMMANDER OUT."

USS Midway

Commodore Prentice readied himself to leave the bridge. Commander Cross met him near the console.

"Commodore," he whispered so that no one else would hear. "I thought I should let you know that communications picked up some more intermittent signals, if you know what I mean."

"What kind of signals?"

"A lone aircraft. Two hundred knots. Angels nine. Fifty miles southeast of our present position and heading one-seven-zero. It's on our radar now. I didn't want to say anything on the intercom. I thought I should contact you in person."

"Good," Prentice whispered back. "Are you saying it's the *Mary Jane*?"

"Yes, sir, I am. What should we do?"

"Have you established radio contact?"

"No, sir."

"Good. Don't! We're heading back to port. We already lost a damn good navy pilot. Ignore it!"

"Aye, aye, sir. If we can."

"Just do it."

Sixteen

Tiger was a free man inside Japanese territory. But for how long?

The warmth of the day was enough to make the pilot zip down the chest part of his flight suit. He stamped in and out of the trees until he spotted a house on a low rise. He removed his helmet and held it, wiping his brow.

To the right was the small field he had spotted from the air. He approached the house cautiously, staying low. At a distance of eighty feet or so, he stopped cold. A white-haired man appeared by an open sliding door. He strolled slowly to the railing and looked about. Tiger lay flat out on the ground, his eyes on the house. A woman joined the man and bowed to him. Then the two went inside and closed the door.

Advancing on the house, Tiger heard aircraft. He squatted down behind a tree, twenty feet from the building. Three Zeros in a tight V-formation cruised overhead and vanished as quickly as they came on the scene. *Patrol planes searching for him?* The old man came out again, glanced skyward, then across his property.

Tiger tried to be as quiet as possible, but when he went to move his right leg, a branch beneath his boot snapped. The old man heard it and looked over. He called to someone inside. Two women appeared through the door. All three took a set of steps down to the ground and walked towards the noise the old man had heard.

Once they got closer, Tiger stood and moved out directly in front of them.

145

Captain Clayton informed the crew that the bomber was now outside enemy fighter range, and that they could relax.

Gabriel Schwartz began to fall asleep in the tail.

Mark Crosby lit up a cigarette and leaned back in his chair. He had done his job, but too bad it had gone for naught. It bothered him that they had to abort. He daydreamed about his wife and being home with her. He missed her something fierce. The war would be over soon, and he'd finally see her face to face for the first time in over a year.

Nevin Brown returned to reading his pocket book, listening in his headphones.

Butch Emerson was still shaking after the disarming episode in the bomb bay. The whole ship—the whole mission—fell on his shoulders. Relieved it was over, he could go back to concentrating on his controls. Barring any mishap, they would make it to Tinian, with a few minutes of fuel to spare.

Paul Lunsford and Carl Loran were still feeling frustrated that the mission hadn't materialized. They both wondered if someone had infiltrated the mission—someone other than Ainsworth—and had the atomic strike canceled. Clayton convinced the crew, however, that they had no choice but to obey orders and abort. The codename—*Electron*—was given and that was that!

Dwight Marshall busied himself plotting the course home. "NAVIGATOR TO COMMANDER. TURN THREE DEGREES LEFT FOR CORRECTION," he said into the intercom. "ONE HOUR AND FIFTEEN MINUTES TO IWO JIMA." He then returned to his log notes.

Just then, the bomber lurched, as if it hit an air pocket. Brown heard a strong radio station that made him sit up.

He listened for several seconds, then contacted Clayton. "RADIO TO COMMANDER."

"COMMANDER HERE."

"I JUST HEARD A RADIO REPORT. THERE'S A TYPHOON WARNING FOR THE MARIANAS."

"WHAT RADIO STATION? OUT HERE?"

"SOUNDS WEIRD TO ME, TOO, SIR. BUT SHE'S COMING IN STRONG." The bomber hit another air pocket. "WHOOPS, THERE IT GOES. I CAN'T GET IT ANYMORE. ISN'T THAT THE GOOFIEST."

146

Clayton shook his head. What was with these air pockets all day? "I GUESS THE WORST ISN'T OVER YET. THANKS NEVIN."

GUAM

Cameron and Robert entered the busy grocery store to stock up for the arrival of Typhoon Matilda. They were staying, although Denise and Edna had already flown out. The other Agana shoppers had the same idea as the two war vets. Robert had a transistor radio with him and listened as they turned into the first aisle.

"Listen to this, Phil," Robert said, turning the volume up.

According to the weather report, the eye of the storm was within 400 miles of Guam. An immediate typhoon watch was declared. The two men looked at each other, concerned. This did not necessarily mean that Guam was in any immediate danger, the announcer went on to say, but it was a possibility. The movements of typhoons were always unpredictable. The eye was centered on the island of Pulap, Caroline Islands, to the southeast, where winds were reaching 135 miles per hour ahead of the storm, 120 miles per hour around the center, and the waves were reaching forty feet in height. To add to it all, eight inches of rain had pelted the island in only a few hours. The islanders were advised to stay tuned for the next advisory and be prepared to act if the watch was updated to a warning.

The trouble with warnings was that they could come a precious few hours before the typhoon's advance, making it too late to snap up any emergency items. Les had experienced a typhoon already and he knew that once a watch became a warning, no one would find a flashlight battery or candle anywhere on the island. That's why he had told his guests to get moving now, even before the watch was officially announced.

Robert turned the radio off and placed it in the buggy. Cameron leaned over Robert's shoulder and checked the list that Gail had written for them. It was plain to see the groceries had to meet three major requirements. First, they shouldn't have to be refrigerated. Second, they shouldn't need to be cooked at all or very little. Third, nothing that would make people thirsty. So salty items were *out*. Luncheon meats, tuna, salmon, unsalted crackers, canned fruits, chocolate bars were *in*. Also listed were batteries, paper cups and plates, plastic forks, spoons, and knives. At the bottom of the list was. . . *Fill car up with gas!* They had already done that.

"I'll get the utensils, Bob. I saw them at the front of the store when we came in."

"Thanks."

Cameron walked to the front and looked out the long glass window. Outside, the palm trees were swaying. The winds were gusting. At last report, seventy miles per hour. The sky loomed dark over Agana. Some rain was falling. Cameron bent down to a lower shelf and grabbed a small box of assorted cutlery and a package of thick cardboard plates. Although paper towels weren't on the list, he snatched two rolls on his way back to the cart.

"Quite the vacation we're having," he said to Robert.

"Yeah."

"You know, come to think of it, I can't remember the last time I went grocery shopping."

"Me neither," Robert chuckled.

Half an hour later, they placed the groceries in the back of Gail's station wagon, struggling against the strong winds. During the drive to Les's house, Cameron, in the passenger seat, remembered a lecture he had given to high school kids a year ago. How ironic. He told the audience that the Hiroshima atomic blast was equal to 20,000 tons of TNT. But that was nothing compared to an average-sized hurricane or typhoon, which was the equivalent of 500,000 Hiroshima atomic bombs. The reason a tropical storm did not result in as much damage as a nuclear blast, he had said, was that a storm was spread out over a large area, perhaps three or four hundred miles and not concentrated on one "ground zero." But, all the same, what power! And here he was in the middle of a typhoon.

Les and Gail were very organized. By the time Robert and Cameron had delivered the groceries into the kitchen, the young couple had deployed the emergency preparations. They had various containers filled with water and stationed at areas throughout the house. Even the bathtub was filled to the top. They weren't taking any chances. In a matter of hours the city's water supply could be contaminated by flooding—by either salt water or sewage—or be cut off entirely. On the kitchen counter were two flashlights, another battery-operated radio, a

148

kerosene lamp, and a half-dozen tall candles. In the basement, where the group would weather the typhoon if it reached Guam, was a supply of toilet paper and two covered pails lined with plastic sheets—the emergency sanitary facilities.

Les helped with the first set of groceries bags, then said to his father and Cameron, "The latest weather advisory from the Typhoon Center has just updated the storm to a watch."

"Here we go," Robert replied.

JAPAN

The nearest person to Tiger was a young girl about fourteen. The old man stepped in front of her and looked the pilot up and down, while another girl, who had to be about eighteen, stayed back some feet.

"You are American," the old man said in English, with a heavy Japanese accent.

Tiger gripped his helmet. "Yes, I am. And you speak English."

"Come quickly, they are searching the countryside."

It was not the kind of reaction that Tiger expected. Neither was what happened next. He was led to the entrance, asked to remove his shoes, then was whisked through the front door and into a room, where the door was closed behind him. Tiger heard talking beyond the walls. He slid to the floor, leaned against the wall and rested his head on his knees. He was alone and very tired.

But, for some off reason, his mind was in high gear, working a mile a minute. The house and surroundings were no different than the few Japanese homes he had been in during his recent stationing in Japan. Recent in 1990, that is. Things had not changed much in forty-five years. In fact, some things had not changed much in centuries. The Japanese were extremely traditional people.

Despite the outdoor heat, it was surprisingly cool inside the house. Several paintings hung on the walls. They were the typical unshadowed scenes of hills, seas, rice fields, cherry and plum trees. The architecture was simple. The wooden house was built around an inner court. Sliding screens made of wood and paper separated rooms. The floors were covered with tightly woven straw mats. There was a low table in Tiger's room, surrounded by several cushions. Bright and medium-toned country scenes were imprinted on the walls.

Tiger fell asleep for a few minutes until he heard a muffled, heavy knock at the front door. With nowhere to go, Tiger listened to the voices of Japanese men. He then heard the old man reply. A few minutes later, the room door slid open, and the two girls and the old man appeared. They all bowed. The old man smiled. The older girl set a tray of food on the table. All three wore the traditional kimono, a long robe with flowing sleeves that was tied at the waist. The girls had high cheekbones, dark eyes, light brown skin, and shiny black hair. The old man was probably in his sixties, what Tiger would probably call the typical Confucius type—very little hair, long stringy beard, with skin as pale as a cloud.

"You must be hungry. My daughters have prepared a tray for you," he said, while he and the older girl smiled.

"Why are you doing this?"

The old man made a quick bow. "You eat now and we talk later." He glanced at the girls and the three left, the younger girl closing the sliding door behind her.

On the tray was a cup of some green tea and small bowls of rice, cooked fish, bean soup, and vegetables. The only utensils were chopsticks. Luckily for Tiger, he knew how to use them. He found everything tasty and devoured it all. Moments later, the younger girl entered the room, bowed, and took the tray out.

Then the old man appeared. He sat on one of the cushions. "I am Saburo Chuichi. I live here with my daughters. And what is your name?"

"Lieutenant Jack Runsted, United States Navy. My friends call me Tiger."

"You Americans enjoy nicknames."

"Why didn't you turn me in?"

"It would serve no purpose. The war will be over soon. My son is in the government. He told me that atomic bombs were dropped on Hiroshima and Nagasaki. Out government will surrender, within days, once the militants in the imperial cabinet realize that the fight is over.

"The Americans will be our conquerors soon. Therefore, to mistreat or turn in any American flier at this time would be pointless. Earlier in the war, I would have sent for the authorities. We only obey orders. Our superiors are supposed to know what's best. But that will change with the coming of the Americans. My son told me that our coal production is down one-eighth of what it is prior to the war. That is not good with winter approaching. Our cities have been destroyed. Millions of homes. Over one million men have been killed in this fight and nearly the same amount of civilians have perished in bombings. We have been fighting a war on a lie. We are not a superior race who had to rule the world. Our past is now in ruins." The old man sighed, then added, "You have permission to stay here in hiding until the end is official."

"Thank you."

Tiger didn't know what to make of it. But the old man had hit the nail on the head when he mentioned that the Americans would soon be the conquerors. History told Tiger that General MacArthur, the Supreme Commander of Allied Powers, would rule Japan as an absolute military ruler through to 1950. MacArthur would be the protector of the Japanese people, while they got back on their feet, and it would be his influence that quickly brought democracy to Japan.

"How do I know I can trust you?" Tiger asked.

Saburo smiled. "As you say in America, you have no choice."

"True. But if they catch me, you and your daughters will be punished."

"I doubt very much the men will return, at least not for a day or so. If they do return, it might be to tell me the war is over, perhaps."

"Perhaps. You have an excellent command of the English language. How is that?"

"I learned it on my own. I also know German, French, and a little Russian."

"You seem to know a lot about Americans."

"I used to teach physics at Tokyo University, until I retired in 1938. My students came from all over the world, including the United States. I see your government has beaten our government in splitting the atom."

"Yes, we have."

"Your flight gear is of an interesting design, especially your helmet. That was your jet aircraft that flew over today, wasn't it? I didn't know the American military had jet aircraft."

"We have now."

"Yes, you do. Very impressive. I taught the theories of jet propulsion in my classes. It's really quite simple, is it not? A blown-up balloon makes an excellent working model. When the balloon's mouth is closed, the air inside pushed in all directions with the same pressure. When the mouth is opened, the air pressure is less at the mouth. However, at the opposite end of the mouth the air pushed with greater pressure. The balloon will then move in the direction of the greatest pressure, which is forward. In conclusion, it is not the exhaust but the forward push with propels the balloon. Simple. Your technicians must have capitalized on it before the rest of the world. We have our Baka bombs which are jet powered, but we don't have a workable fighter or bomber."

Saburo watched Tiger yawning. "I'm sorry to bore you. You must know how a jet works, otherwise you wouldn't be flying one. I see you are tired. My daughter has started a hot bath for you in the next room. A hot bath and a good sleep will cure your ills."

Tiger smiled. "It will indeed, sir. Thank you."

"Come."

Moments later, Tiger eased his sore and tired body into the steaming, almost scalding, hot water of the sunken tub. The Japanese version of a hot tub. To one side were towels, neatly stacked. The water was such a relief that he laid his head back and went to sleep.

Kyoto

David drove straight to Toshika's apartment complex and took the elevator to the third floor. He knocked four times in rapid succession at her door.

The door opened slowly, the chain lock still on. Her face flushed, Toshika peeked through the small opening.

"Toshika, please let me in. It's important."

"After what you made me do!"

"What?"

Toshika was in tears. "Colonel Mason had a heart attack today."

"He did?"

"That little session of yours about the codename was probably too much for him. He may not make it through the night. And for what? Something that happened nearly fifty years ago. I told you on the phone I wanted to be alone."

"All the more reason to see you. I have something to tell you that will explain everything. Please."

"Oh, all right," she said, wiping the tears from her eyes with her hand. She removed the chain and David entered.

"Here, read this. I just got it two hours ago. Sit down. Relax." He handed her a ripped-open envelope with a PRIORITY stamp on it, then headed to her liquor cabinet. Inside the envelope was a typed piece of paper, a US Navy dispatch on a proper letterhead from the commanding officer of the carrier USS *Midway*. She sat on the couch and read the first sentence.

FOLLOWING THE READING OF THIS DISPATCH, PLEASE DESTROY AND DO NOT REVEAL THE CONTENTS TO ANYONE.

"David, it's addressed to you and it says that no one else is–"
"Never mind that." David poured vodka and lime juice into a glass. "You were involved and you have to know. The wrath of the US Navy if I do tell you is nothing compared to your wrath if I don't tell you. Read on." Then he poured a second drink.

YOU WERE GIVEN THE JOB OF FINDING THE CODENAME FOR A REASON THAT FOR SECURITY REASONS I CAN'T DIVULGE. HOW YOU EVER STUMBLED ONTO MASON WAS A STROKE OF LUCK AT A TIME WHEN WE NEEDED IT. YOU DID A GREAT SERVICE TO YOUR COUNTRY AND THE WORLD. THE MISSION IN QUESTION DID NOT EXIST. DO I MAKE MYSELF CLEAR? MANY THANKS. COMMODORE PRENTICE. USS MIDWAY.

Toshika's tears stopped in an instant once she read the dispatch. "David, what's going on?"
"Let's not ask."
"I'm so sorry for how I acted, David."
"Forget it." He walked over to her, a drink in both hands, giving her one. "Now, to something else. I want to ask you a simple question." He sat on the couch with her, the paper falling to the floor. "A drink to us."
"What's this all about?"
They sipped their drinks. David set his glass on the nearby table.
"Will you marry me?"
Toshika sat speechless. "I don't. . . know what to–"
"Just say, yes. That's all I want to hear."
"You're not proposing just to shut me up about the *Mary Jane* mission, are you?"
He laughed. "It did cross my mind. No, of course not."

"It that case, I say. . . yes."

Then. . . the doorbell rang just as they were about to kiss.

"I'll flush the dispatch down the toilet while you answer it," Toshika said.

"Sure."

David got up and stared into the peephole. At first he thought he was seeing things. The toilet flushed and David heard Toshika approaching.

"Well," she said, "who is it?"

"I don't believe it."

The doorbell rang again.

"It's my mother. Here! Now!"

"Let her in."

David swung the door open. "Mom, what are you doing here?" He looked down the hall. "Where's dad?"

"Still on Guam. I just got off the plane. Your butler told me where you were. Don't just stand there. Let me in."

David and Edna hugged at the door, while Toshika closed it.

"Mom, I'd like you to meet Toshika Ushida, my. . . my fiancée. I just proposed a minute ago, actually."

"Aren't you the sly one? That's great!" Edna embraced Toshika.

All three settled on the couch.

"I know dad won't approve," David chuckled.

"Ah, to hell with him."

"But you're the one who has to live with the guy."

"Leave it to me."

"So, why is dad still on Guam?"

"He and Phil Cameron are sticking it out with Les and the family until the typhoon passes."

"Geez, that's kind of dangerous, isn't it?"

"I know. But they're taking the precautions. Denise, Cameron's wife, flew back to California today. I came here. Your dad will join us later. Maybe Les, Gail, and the kids, too."

David sighed. "I sure hope so."

"They better be careful," Toshika added.

The other two could only nod.

Seventeen

As Matilda neared Guam, the typhoon watch turned to a typhoon warning.

The weather forecasters believed that in a matter of hours Matilda, with all its fury, would smash into the island. High winds, high water, and rough seas were predicted.

Although several Guam residents who thought the eye of the storm would miss them were caught off guard, the Shilling household were swinging into action. Because the house was on higher ground and not along the coast, Cameron and the Shillings didn't have to worry about the rising water of the storm wave. Their main concerns would be the wind and the rain.

Cameron and Robert boarded up the windows firmly and brought everything from the yard into the house. Les turned off the water heater and the gas at the main inlet. He also unplugged everything electrical except for the freezer, the fridge, the radio, and the television.

Over the radio, Cameron heard that the storm would probably approach the island from the southeast. Therefore, he opened two windows on the east side to act as a release valve inside the house. Immediately, a strong, howling, damp wind greeted him. Looking up, he saw that the sky was a fierce gray.

*J*APAN

Tiger woke up, the second time in an hour that he had fallen asleep. He was still in the sunken tub and the water was still quite warm. He

155

slid up, rubbed his eyes, and spread his arms on the sides of the tub, his eyes on the door.

"Hello, lieutenant." Saburo bowed and entered the room. "I was beginning to think you had drowned. Did you sleep well?"

"For not being a bed, I slept very well, thank you. It felt so good, I couldn't stay awake."

"I heard some talk in the village. Were you the one who destroyed the planes at the base?"

"Yes, I was."

"It seems several guards are searching the countryside. They are looking for the man in the magic machine, as they call it. You hurt the pride of the base."

"How did I do that?"

"By destroying the new elite Zero squadron. They are long-range fighters with drop tanks. The pilots are in training to attack Superfortresses before they approach our mainland."

Tiger perked up. "Did you say, long-range. How long of range?"

"They can fly to Iwo Jima and back, I'm told."

"Is that so?" Tiger calculated in his mind. . . *1,500 miles one way.* Could he still catch the *Mary Jane*? It was worth a try. "How far is it to the base?"

"Oh, ten miles."

"What's the quickest way of getting there?"

Saburo held a finger up. "Ah, you're planning an escape, are you?"

"You bet I am."

"I know a farmer down the road. You could use his truck. But I would have to get it first. How do you plan to get past the search parties?"

"I'll find some way."

"Get dressed, wait in your room, and I'll be back shortly."

The older girl appeared with some work clothes, a shirt, a pair of dark slacks, and a pair of well-worn shoes. Once Saburo and his daughter left, Tiger threw on the clothes and returned to his room, where he waited for twenty minutes. Then, to his shock, he heard shouting. Men's voices. Tiger had no place to go, no place to hide.

The screen shot open with a hard bang. Two machine-gun-toting guards stood at the door, their barrels held on Tiger. One of the men threw Tiger's flight suit, boots, and helmet at him. Tiger got the picture. *Put them on!* Behind the guards he heard more shouting from other men, interspaced with screams from the girls. Saburo and his daughters were brought into the hall opposite the opening to the room. Tiger stripped down to his underwear and slid into the flight gear and boots. With two guns at his back, he walked through the entrance, his head held high.

His eyes met Saburo's. Tiger bowed and continued on, down the hall and out into the bright sunshine. He saw two brown army trucks ahead. Two guard dogs were tied to the driver's door handle. To either side of the narrow, gravel roadway were thick trees.

Then. . . a noisy aircraft—a Zero—flew low over head.

The guards looked up. Tiger darted off to the right, into the thick trees and ran, finally stopping a few minutes later to catch his breath. *No one behind him.* But he could hear the dogs barking. And they didn't sound that far off. He kept running. The forest was thick, but it couldn't keep him hidden for very long. For one of the few times in his life, he was truly scared. He knew what the Japanese authorities did to shot-down American airmen during World War Two. They had no mercy.

Coming to a short open field, he saw a ragged path a hundred feet off, leading from the field on the other side back into the forest. He took off on a dead run and made it to the path, just as two guards appeared at the edge of the forest. He turned and saw a flash from one of the guns.

Tiger hit the dirt, a stinging pain in his left leg. Bleeding from his ankle, he crawled, then ran as best he could from their sight into the forest. After fifty feet, he gave up. He dropped on the spot, beside a tree trunk, where he turned and waited. The guards ran up, shoving the rifle butts into his chest.

"All right, assholes, knock it off!"

The dogs barked fiercely, showing sharp teeth. The guards looked down at Tiger. One of them shouted and motioned to Tiger to get up. The guards blindfolded him and ordered him to walk the entire distance to Saburo's house, punching him and prodding him along the way with the rifle butts.

They stopped at the truck, where Tiger was pushed into the back and was kept under guard for a slow, thirty-minute trip. Then his blindfold was ripped off and he was grabbed from the back of the truck. Facing him was a small, rod-bearing Japanese officer in glasses. Tiger looked around and saw the base he had shot up. He smiled when he saw the blackened remains of the fighters off to one side of the hangar.

The officer shouted in Japanese and some guards rushed forward to tie Tiger's hands behind him. He was forced to walk again. On the way, he saw three Zeros off to the left, drop tanks attached to the bottom fuselage. The guards flung him into a room inside a small building. A large, tough-looking thug stared at him, as one guard dropped him on a chair. The officer stepped forward and stood over Tiger.

"All right, Joe, name, rank, and serial number," the officer demanded in English.

"My name is not Joe," Tiger replied. "And I need a doctor."

"Every American is Joe to me." The officer struck Tiger across the face with the rod. "Name, rank, serial number!"

Tiger felt a line of blood trickling down his cheek. "My name is Joe, United States–"

"Your real name!"

"I thought you decided my name is Joe."

"Name, rank, serial number!"

"Lieutenant Jack Runsted, United States Navy. Number 565675."

The officer pointed his stick toward the door. "That was some exhibition you put on out there today."

"Fucking right it was."

The officer caught the smirk on Tiger's face and struck him again with the rod, this time on the shoulder. "What kind of aircraft were you flying?"

Tiger flinched and said, "I'm only required to give my name, rank, and serial number."

"You're one of those smart-ass Joes."

"My name is Jack."

One of the guards brought in Tiger's helmet and oxygen mask and placed it on a long table. The officer looked at the pieces, and was especially interested in the darkened visor and padded lining. "What does Tiger stand for?" he asked, reading the name on the front.

"My nickname."

The officer then eyed Tiger's flight suit, poking the ankle and shoulder pockets. "Where did you come from? What base?"

Oh, what the hell, Tiger thought. Keeping military secrets now wouldn't mean anything.

"A carrier."

"Which one?"

"USS Midway."

"Never heard of it."

"It's our. . . newest."

"What kind of jet-propulsion aircraft were you flying?"

Tiger smiled. "The best. F-18 Hornet."

"What engines were you using?"

"Twin turbofans. Sixteen thousand pounds of thrust. It can go twice the speed of sound."

"Twice the speed of sound! That's impossible! I want the truth!"

"It is the truth. Why would I lie? You saw what it could do." *Thanks to some 1990 Japanese computer technology*, Tiger wanted to say. "You were lucky. If you hadn't got a piece of me, I would have wiped out your whole base."

"Where is your fighter now?"

"The bottom of the ocean."

"Why are you so eager to answer my questions?"

Tiger held his head up. "Because Japan has lost the war. Your government will surrender within seventy-two hours. So you had better be good to me, pal."

"Lies! All lies!" The officer brought the rod up to strike Tiger again, but didn't.

Tiger was trying to loosen the rope of his tied hands. "You must know by now that Hiroshima and Nagasaki were destroyed a few days ago by two powerful atomic bombs."

The officer pulled back. "How did you know?"

"I know."

"What was your mission to our country?"

"Escort the third atomic mission."

"Another one!"

"Yes."

"The target. Give me the target!"

"Kyoto."

"You wouldn't dare."

"We didn't think you'd bomb Pearl Harbor."

The officer spun around and said something to the guard at the door. The guard turned the handle and left.

Tiger winced. "May I have a doctor now?"

"Not until you answer more questions."

"Shoot. I mean. . . go ahead."

Tiger's interrogation continued. All the answers he gave either puzzled or angered the officer. Then a doctor arrived and bandaged Tiger's ankle. It was only a flesh wound—the bullet had grazed Tiger's ankle—but he had lost a lot of blood. The officer left for five minutes, then returned with fire in his eyes. By that time, Tiger was nearly free of his rope.

"You are a liar, Joe! There was no attack on Kyoto! It is still standing. Where was the real attack? Answer me, Joe."

Tiger realized now that the bomb didn't go off. *Thank God.* Then something else occurred to him. *Was it dropped in 1990?*

The officer struck Tiger twice more on the shoulder. Then he stepped back and stomped to the door. Before leaving the room, he nodded at the muscle man.

GUAM

Cameron and the Shillings cramped themselves into the Shilling's basement. Outside, the typhoon raged, making its landfall in the afternoon. Winds of more than a hundred miles per hour and a wall of rain slammed the city and the island of Guam. Electricity went first. The winds howled on for a few hours. Then the wind and rain died off. Suddenly, the sun shone through a crack in one of the boarded-up basement windows.

"It stopped," Cameron noted with wonder. "And the sun's shining."

"Let's go topside," Robert suggested.

Les went outside with the men. They walked down the driveway and had a look at the neighborhood. Some trees had been uprooted, but the houses were generally intact, except for a few smashed windows, scattered debris in the yards, and a couple dented cars. Every roof had hung on. Les's yard stood untouched. The air had a slight breeze to it, maybe five knots, and the temperature seemed warm.

Les studied the sky. In every direction, he saw a barrier of ominous cloud. "We're surrounded. We're in the eye."

Robert and Cameron saw it too.

"It's not over yet," Cameron said.

"Not by a long shot," Les replied. "We only got a few minutes, maybe an hour before the winds hit us from the opposite direction. The next time around it may be worse."

Eighteen

As the thug stepped closer, Tiger sprang up and with all the strength he could muster in his good leg kicked the man in the testicles so hard that he buckled over in pain. Two more kicks to the face knocked him unconscious. Tiger wanted to strangle the man with the rope for good measure, but threw it on the floor instead.

Tiger ran to the door and out towards the back of the building. He bolted for two sets of long hangars and slid down low to the ground once he was out in the open. The closest Japs, three mechanics four planes to his right, were busy working on a fighter. Tiger had only one hundred feet to crawl to the nearest Zero. He half-ran, half-crawled to it, making it there in seconds.

Tiger jumped on the wing of the Zero and threw himself into the cockpit. He had never flown a Zero before in his life. Or any vintage World War Two plane, for that matter. But compared to an F-18, he didn't figure he'd have a problem. He scanned the gauges. *Yeah. . . no problem*. His left hand went for the primer on the bottom left and then his right hand hit the ignition switch on the bottom right. The three-bladed prop begin to rotate, and smoke belched out the exhaust as the radial engine caught fire. He advanced the throttle and watched the gauges slowly spring to life. The fuselage, wing, and auxiliary tanks were topped to full. Perfect. He knew he couldn't afford the luxury of waiting for the oil pressure and cylinder head temperature rise to the proper limits. He had to move out. *Now*.

The three mechanics ran towards him. Tiger advanced the throttle and released the brakes, taking a sharp turn down the dispersal track. Two of the men scrambled out of the way of the spinning prop, but the third man jumped on the trailing edge of the port wing. He desperately hung on, as Tiger, trying to shake him, pressed his feet on the rudders, which cause the Zero to zigzag back and forth. It was no use. The Jap worked his way forward as Tiger picked up speed. He then gripped the edge of the windscreen, ready to punch Tiger in the open cockpit. Tiger slammed the Jap's hand until it was a bloody piece of flesh. A quick turn at the edge of the runway managed to fling the Jap off. There he left him lying on the pavement. Out cold.

Tiger didn't notice what direction the wind was coming from and at this point couldn't make any adjustments because there was no windsock. Whether he was about to take off downwind was only a technicality. At the other end of the runway, he saw some trucks and men working into position in an attempt to cut off his path of escape.

The instrument temperatures were rising. . . finally. He dropped the flaps and flicked the ammo button on the stick. The machine gun was live. He pushed the throttle to maximum and let the brakes go. *He was off.* Across the base, men were running out of buildings. Down the far end of the runway, three trucks were coming towards him. Tiger raced at them head on. As he lifted the Zero's tail, he squeezed off several rounds of 7.7mm shells at the trucks to scare them off. It worked. They all stopped.

At less than 500 yards from the lead truck, Tiger still hadn't the proper lift for takeoff. He saw a soldier jump from the third truck and squat down to aim his rifle. Tiger scrunched down behind the instrument panel. Luckily, the soldier was a bad shot. Nothing made contact. The gap was less than 200 yards by the time Tiger heaved back the column and lifted off the runway. *Landing gear.* He pressed a lever on his right and the undercarriage banged into the belly.

Tiger flinched.

Damn! He was going to hit the trucks. He closed his eyes. . . and flew so low over the trucks that the men were forced to duck.

MARY JANE

Gabriel Schwartz, in a dreamy state of half-consciousness, began to fall asleep in the tail section. He had felt the bomber descending for several minutes now. They were almost home. *There... off to the side.* He jolted awake. Did he really see it? A Japanese Zero fighter?

He sat up and looked around. Nothing but clouds. Thick, heavy clouds. What would a Zero be doing out anyway? There were no enemy bases this close to the Marianas. Wait a minute. Clouds? Where did they come from?

Then... *he did see it.* It was a Zero. Below to port. Flying meatball and all, bursting through the clouds. Schwartz quickly aimed his guns at the fighter and fired off a few rounds as the Zero whizzed past underneath.

"TAIL GUNNER TO COMMANDER. A ZERO JUST FLEW UNDER US."

"A ZERO? WAY IN THE HELL OUT HERE?"

"YES, SIR."

"YUH SURE IT WAS A ZERO?"

"POSITIVE."

In the cockpit, Loran pointed down to his right, his face to the cockpit glass. "I see it. Banking into a cloud bank."

Ian kept looking straight ahead. "This is screwy."

He observed the massive cloud formation a few miles above the bomber, cloud layers stacked tier upon tier in circular arrangements. This had to be the typhoon his radio operator warned him about. What a dumb time to hit... during their descent to Tinian. Soon, the *Mary Jane* was engulfed in cloud that faded from white to gray in seconds. The machine rocked and shook. Lightning flashed. Thunder exploded. Rain and hail pelted the metal skin.

"COMMANDER TO RADIO OPERATOR." Clayton's voice vibrated with the constant jitter now pounding the bomber. "ANY RADIO CONTACT WITH TINIAN?"

"NOTHING, COMMANDER. THE STORM MUST HAVE KNOCKED OUT ALL COMMUNICATION."

"TRY GUAM."

"I DID ALREADY. NOTHING THERE EITHER. WE'RE DEAD IN THE WATER."

"NAVIGATOR TO COMMANDER."

"I HEAR YUH. I HOPE YOU HAVE SOME GOOD NEWS."

"NOT REALLY. I DON'T KNOW WHERE WE ARE. NOTHING'S READING. MY COMPASS IS ALL HAYWIRE."

"Look, Ian!" Loran shouted, pointing at the cockpit instruments.

Every dial and instrument was spinning madly, almost out of control.

Clayton remembered the last altitude check showed 8,000 feet, and he knew he had descended even lower than that. What a ride! Zero visibility. Altimeter going nuts.

"RADAR, CAN YOU GIVE US A BEARING?"

"I'M KNOCKED OUT TOO, COMMANDER. SORRY."

Clayton turned and shouted to his flight engineer. "Butch!"

"Yes, sir."

"How much fuel do we have left?"

"Twenty-five minutes, if we're lucky."

Paul Lunsford leaned forward from the nose. "Captain, I've got an idea?"

"Let's hear it," Clayton answered, hanging on the controls.

"Let's climb out of this mess and look for the center. I once read somewhere that the eye is supposed to be the calmest part of any hurricane or typhoon. Let's find the eye and see if she's over land. If not, we'll follow it until it is over land. And hopefully one of our bomber bases."

Loran shrugged. "Sounds OK by me."

"Let's do it," Clayton said, pulling up on the controls. The *Mary Jane* climbed skyward, the four radial engines straining. The dark-gray cloud turned to a lighter gray. Like magic, the instruments returned to normal. The sun burst through. Then, they were above the cloud. The altimeter read 32,000 feet.

"RADAR OPERATOR TO COMMANDER. I GOT A READING OF A COAST-LINE BELOW US THROUGH ALL THAT. BY THE SHAPE OF IT, THOUGH, SHE'S NOT TINIAN."

"There it is, captain!" Lunsford shouted. "Through some scattered cloud."

"Where?"

"Off starboard."

"Yeah," Clayton nodded. "Butch, how much fuel?"

"Ten, maybe fifteen minutes, tops."

The cloud below thinned out. The air was calm. It was an awesome sight. Any of the crew members who had a window watched in awe at the circular wall of cloud that surrounded them, three or four miles higher than their altitude.

"Holy shit! That's Guam!" Loran shouted. "The eye is over Guam. Hot damn! That looks like the navy base at Agana. Geez, those runways are too small, though. We have to make North Field where the B-29 base is."

"Too late," Clayton said, pointing in the direction of the base. "Look, North Field is too close to the storm wall. It's the navy base, short runways or no short runways."

"You're right."

Clayton banked left and began to descend quickly. "COMMANDER TO RADIO OPERATOR. CAN YOU MAKE RADIO CONTACT?"

"I'M RUNNING THROUGH THE FREQUENCIES NOW, SIR."

AGANA

Captain MacDonald and a skeleton crew had kept the base open through the first stage of the typhoon, weathering it out in the administration building. Now, in the eye, MacDonald came out for air, standing on the steps of the building, scanning the base. Startled, he heard prop engines overhead and glanced up. *What! Who the hell was out in this!* At first the sight of a four-engined B-29 circling on final approach—gear down—didn't register. As it kept banking, it was then that he clearly saw eight letters on the shiny metal surface below the port window.

What the... *Crap!* It was the *Mary Jane*.

Aboard the *Mary Jane*, Clayton aimed the nose for the very edge of the nearest runway so that he would have plenty of room to slow down at the other end. If he could.

"Wing flaps, forty-five degrees."

Loran's left hand went for the aisle stand where the switches for the landing sequence were situated. "Wing flaps, forty-five degrees."

"COMMANDER TO RADIO OPERATOR. RETRACT ANTENNA."

"ROGER, COMMANDER."

Clayton nodded. By experience, Loran knew what that nod meant, and his hand went again to the aisle stand, this time for the automatic flight control system. He flicked the switch to OFF.

"COMMANDER TO ENGINEER. MIXTURE?"

"AUTO-RICH."

"BOOSTER PUMPS?"

"ON."

"FUEL PRESSURE?"

"SIXTEEN INCHES, COMMANDER."

Loran moved the supercharger controls to ON and the propeller controls to a cruise speed of 2,000 RPM. At the same time, he carefully watched the speed as the ground and runway raced towards them.

"Speed 130, Ian... 125..."

MacDonald ran into the administration building and burst into his office.

"Tower!" he belted into the telephone receiver. "This is Captain MacDonald."

"Yes, sir."

"What's the B-29 doing out there?"

"He said it's an emergency, sir. He said he has to land. He only has ten minutes or less of fuel."

"What was his callsign?"

"Hawkeye three-six."

"Oh, no! Stop him!" MacDonald demanded.

"I can't, sir. It just landed."

MacDonald slammed the receiver down, then picked it up again and tapped out another number. It rang twice before someone answered.

"Security."

"This is Captain MacDonald. I want two of your men to meet me in front of the runway side of the administration building in one minute, with a jeep and guns loaded. Got that?"

"Yes, sir."

Clayton feathered the brakes, pressing harder each time, as the end of the runway loomed closer. Finally, he was forced to press all the way.

"Come on, *Mary Jane*, stop. STOP!"

MacDonald sprinted down the hall, and by the time he flew out the door the jeep was waiting for him.

"Follow that bomber!" he yelled, out of breath, at the driver.

"Aye, aye, captain."

At the end of the runway, the tired crew tramped down the nose hatch and walked free of the bomber. They had come to a stop only fifteen feet short of the runway's edge.

"Where are we, Ian?" Loran asked. "I thought this was Guam."

"Look over there," Clayton said, pointing across the runway. "More of those strange fighters with no props."

Schwartz felt for the film he had removed from the camera. It was still inside his breast pocket. His eyes went to the black skid marks down the runway. "What a ride that was!"

"Hey," Marshall called out, "here comes a jeep."

"Man alive, that's a Superfortress," the jeep driver commented, as he drove closer.

"Stop right here, now!" MacDonald said.

The driver slammed on the brakes sixty feet short of the bomber. MacDonald jumped out, ten feet from the aircrew and pulled a gun on them. Behind him, the two security men held their guns high while they jumped from the jeep. MacDonald stared at the bomber and saw the letters *Mary Jane* below the pilot window and the painting of the busty girl in a green bathing suit. *This wasn't possible. It just wasn't.* "Who's Captain Clayton?" he wanted to know.

"Right here." Clayton stepped forward. "How'd yuh know my name?"

"Never mind that. I know a lot of things about you."

"What is this place? I thought we were landing at Agana."

"Get out of here. Get back in your bomber and GO! Now!"

"Are you kidding?" Clayton shouted back. "Our tanks are nearly bone dry. Where are we supposed to go in this storm? We don't have enough fuel for a proper takeoff!"

"I don't care! Get out of here, or we'll shoot you on the spot." MacDonald couldn't think of what to say next. Then. . . "This is. . . this is a restricted US Navy area. You have no business being here."

The guards pointed their guns at Schwartz and Marshall.

Clayton glanced over his shoulder at his crew. "I think they mean it, boys. Let's go."

"Why did you let us land in the first place?" Loran asked MacDonald.

Nineteen

Les heard the rustle of the palm tree leaves across the street. The wind was coming from the opposite direction and the sky was growing darker by the minute. "We better get back in the house," he said to his father and Cameron. "The calm is over. Here comes the second blast."

No sooner had they returned to the house than the typhoon roared through the neighborhood again, only stronger this time. The house shook and banged from the gusting rain-swept winds. For hours the wind gusts didn't let up. In the evening, the gusts stopped. The wind still howled, but it soon subsided to a strong breeze.

Thirty minutes before nightfall, the Shilling family and Cameron emerged in the drizzling rain to check the damage. Two windows of the house were shattered, the front screen was nowhere to be seen, a backyard palm tree was uprooted and lying against the side of the house, and most of the eaves trough was torn away. They were the lucky ones on the block, though. The street resembled a disaster area. Several houses were demolished. Debris littered the sidewalks and the grass. One car was crushed by the weight of a palm. A few neighbors who had braved the storm were outside in the warm, drizzling rain. Some were crying, most were too shocked to shed tears.

"I hear someone yelling for help! That way!" a neighbor yelled, pointing.

Cameron, Les, and Robert ran three houses down the street. An elderly woman was trapped inside her collapsed living room. It took twenty minutes to remove the wood splinters, but they finally pulled her out, with the help of two other neighbors. Gail ran up with a first-aid kit and two flashlights, handing one to Les, as the woman lay on the grass of her littered property. Darkness had set in now. Several other flashlights were seen up and down the street.

"Les, Captain MacDonald is on the phone," she said, as she tended to the woman.

"For me?"

"Yes, you. He said it was important."

"You mean the telephone lines are working?"

"I guess so."

Back at the house, Les grabbed the receiver off the counter. "Yes, sir."

"Lieutenant, this is Captain MacDonald. Thank God the phones are up. Anyway, can you get over to the base, pronto?"

"Now, sir?"

"Yes, right now."

"But, sir, we're cleaning up. Our neighborhood was hit hard."

"Is your family fine?"

"Yes, they are."

"Good. Lieutenant, this is more important than Matilda. It has to do with the *Mary Jane.*"

"In that case, maybe I should invite General Cameron and my father along."

"What? Are they still on Guam?"

Les chuckled. "We weathered out the storm at the house. All of us."

"You're joking! All of you? Geez, why didn't you go to one of the shelters?"

"There wasn't time, sir."

MacDonald let out a whistle. "Yeah, bring them along too. Right away! I'll wait by my office in the administration building."

MacDonald met them in a long hallway and led them to a restricted area where a guard was posted opposite a door. "You guys won't believe it. I won't say anything else. Just get a load of this."

He opened the door. Inside were eight young men in World War Two flying gear, all watching a video, the sound up high.

"Hi, Phil," one of the men said. "Turn it down, somebody," he demanded.

172

Cameron's mouth began to quiver. Robert held his breath for a moment. Time itself seemed to stop. The two war vets studied each face in the large room. Each person stared back. It was the crew of the *Mary Jane*, all seated on couches, watching a navy video about the F-18 Hornet! Clayton, Marshall, Lunsford, Emerson, Crosby, Schwartz, and Brown.

"I said, turn it down," Clayton repeated, as he stood. "In fact, shut it off. Does somebody know how to do that?"

Marshall reached for the video machine, punched a couple buttons, and pulled the cassette out. "There we go."

"Look who's here," Clayton said, grinning. "It's Bob and Phil."

Robert finally found his voice. "This can't be," he said to MacDonald behind him.

"Oh, but it is," MacDonald replied, letting Les in the room before closing the door.

"What are they doing here?" Cameron asked MacDonald. "Why aren't they back in 1945, where they belong?"

"Geez, those F-18s," Clayton said, wide-eyed. "Jet fighters twice the speed of sound. Remarkable! Look, Phil, we didn't want to believe it, either. That is until Captain MacDonald showed us 1990 calendars, his driver's license, this video, newspapers, magazines, television."

Cameron had a lump in his throat. "How did you guys get here?"

MacDonald tapped the general on the shoulder. "When the typhoon reached the island, lo and behold, there was the *Mary Jane* attempting an emergency landing at our base. Tinian was socked in. The buggers flew right through the typhoon to get here. They had already landed and jumped out when me and two security guards got to the runway. My mind told me one thing—the crew had to return to the *Mary Jane* and take off, otherwise they would never see 1945 again. But before they could, the *Mary Jane* vanished before our eyes, leaving the crew. So, here they are."

Cameron frowned at MacDonald. "That probably explains why the *Mary Jane* was found intact forty-five years ago on Guam, minus the crew."

"Seems so," MacDonald answered.

The reality setting in now, Robert reached out to shake Clayton's hand. "Ian, it's good to see you. But you're still a damn pain in the ass, yuh know that."

Clayton laughed, thinking of the times he had hounded his ground crew. "If this was 1945, I'd have you court-martialed for that, sergeant. Why should you be so happy to see me? It was just twenty-four hours ago that we attended the Kyoto briefing on Tinian."

"But to me that was forty-five years ago," Robert said, stating the obvious.

"True. I see you got a lot of gray hairs. I knew all that hard work and worry about us would take its toll." The others laughed. "And who might you be?" Clayton asked, pointing at Les Shilling.

Les grinned. "Captain Clayton, I'm Lieutenant Les Shilling."

"My son," Robert added.

"I was your escort, sir, over Japan. In the F-18."

"Well, I'll be... All that time, it was Bob's son. Shit!"

"That's quite the fighter," Lunsford said. "And those rockets!"

"AIM-7 Sparrows," Les answered with the proper name.

"I hear they're radar-guided, is that right?"

"Yes, they are."

"You a baseball fan, captain?" Les asked Clayton.

"I am. Why?"

"Remember, you asked me over the radio how many home runs Babe Ruth hit in 1927."

"Yeah, I had to check if you were one of us."

Les smiled. "I'm a baseball fan, too, sir. In 1961, a Yankee outfielder by the name of Roger Maris hit 61 homers to break the Babe's record."

"No kidding. Somebody finally did it."

Then MacDonald opened the door and waved a finger to an NCO down the hall. In seconds, Jack Runsted appeared at the doorway, stepping inside.

"Tiger?" Les said, surprised to see his wingman and so bruised and red-faced. "You're back!"

The two pilots grabbed each other by the shoulders.

"Quite the shock to the system, eh?" Tiger declared. "I see you met the crew."

"Yeah, we did. But you. What the hell happened?"

The pilots released their grip on each other.

"It's like this," Tiger began. "I bailed out near Osaka Bay after shooting up a base. I set the fighter on auto-pilot and sent her out to sea. I got

174

captured by the Japs. After interrogation and a few lumps"—he rubbed the bruises and cuts to his face—"I escaped Japan with a Zero. What a jalopy! But it had the range. They're light as a feather so they hardly use any fuel. I flew the same return course as the *Mary Jane*, hoping to find her. Luckily, I did, before she descended to Tinian. I slid under her and together we came out in 1990, in the middle of the typhoon. By that time I was nearly out of gas and without a parachute. I broke away and plunked her in the water just off a beach near Tinian. The Zero sank, and the air-sea rescue picked me up swimming for shore. I damn near drowned."

Cameron gently put his hand on MacDonald's shoulder. "Can Bob and I see you a moment, captain? Alone."

"Sure, I guess."

Standing in a closed-door, glassed-in room down the hall, Cameron burst out, "What are we going to do with them?"

"It's a navy problem. We'll brief them on what's happened the last forty-five years. They'll be given navy jobs here on Guam, for the time being. After that, I don't know. Eventually, they'll end up in the States. I really don't know. Things like this don't occur every day."

Cameron heaved a sigh. "It's finally over. It took forty-five years to solve the *Mary Jane* mystery, why she was sitting out there in 1945, intact, in the Guam jungle. Wait a sec, the log. Did you get the log from Marshall?"

"I sure as hell did," MacDonald answered. "I know how incriminating it would be with the Kyoto notations in it. I threw it in the incinerator."

"Good idea." Cameron remembered that the log was one of the first items he had searched for aboard the Mary Jane back in 1945. "Hold on. Knowing Marshall, he probably would have plotted the bomb drop. There's a plutonium bomb dropped at the bottom of the Pacific somewhere!"

"I looked through the log before I threw it away and copied down the position. Approximately 200 miles off the Japan coast."

"Yes, but was it dropped in 1945 or 1990?"

"What does that matter?"

"If it was dropped forty-five years ago, then it's certain to be a health hazard today because the salt water will have corroded the casing."

"There's nothing we can do about that, general."

"Hey, I just thought of something," Robert said. "One of the crew members is missing?"

"Who, Bob?"

"Ainsworth, the explosives expert who armed the bomb."

"Yeah, Four Eyes," Cameron said.

"He's dead," MacDonald replied, bluntly. "Shot."

"What!"

"He was a Russian spy, general," MacDonald explained. "According to the crew, he tried to skyjack the *Mary Jane* over Japan by ordering Clayton to fly to Vladivostok. But he didn't get too far. They overpowered him, turned his own gun on him and shot him after he fired a few shots through the fuselage. Then they dumped him out with the unarmed bomb over the ocean."

"He probably made a good meal for the sharks," Cameron chuckled.

"There's something else I better fill you in on, you two. I received a cable just twenty minutes ago from Commodore Prentice in Yokosuka. Colonel Mason died of heart failure. Your son, Mr. Shilling, was lucky to find Mason when he did."

"You're right."

Cameron's thoughts quickly returned to 1945 and the *Mary Jane* in the jungle. The pieces were falling into place. The blood stains and glasses he found were Ainsworth's. He was shot and dragged to the bomb bay. And the rags stuffed into the fuselage metal were not due to an enemy attack. They were from Ainsworth's gun, fired wildly during a struggle. It all made sense now. Except for...

"I have a few questions, captain."

"Go ahead, general."

"When I found the *Mary Jane*, she was resting in jungle just inside the Agana base compound. Where was she when she disappeared in 1990?"

"The far end of one of the runways."

"But–"

"Let me finish. I did some checking. The naval base had one of the runways, the same one *Mary Jane* landed on in 1990, extended some fifteen years ago. You get one guess what the engineers were forced to clear to extend it."

Cameron smirked. "Jungle, I bet."

"Right on, general. That's why she was found undamaged in the jungle in 1945."

"I see. I have another question."

"Shoot."

"The tail gunner–"

"Schwartz?"

"Yes, Gabe Schwartz. Did you grab the film from him?"

"You don't miss a trick, do you? The timing couldn't have been more perfect." MacDonald looked through the glass to the hall and waved a young man to enter. "Here comes our man from the lab right now."

An NCO opened the door and placed a large manila envelope in MacDonald's hand. "Here they are, sir. Where on earth did you find 620 film? That stuff's as old as the hills. Kodak hasn't made it for years. I played around with the developing times a bit. Luckily, it was black and white, where there was lots of room for error. The shots are a bit on the blurry side, but not that bad, I guess."

"Thanks."

The NCO left and MacDonald shut the door. He, Robert and Cameron sat at the table inside. MacDonald pulled out three 8 x 10 black-and-white nose shots of an F-18 Hornet in flight, taken through what appeared to be Plexiglas.

"That's my son's fighter!" Robert exclaimed, catching the callsign HULK on the fuselage.

"In 1945, I found an opened box camera near the *Mary Jane*'s tail gun seat," Cameron recalled. "Just think, if Gabe hadn't removed the film when he and the others left the *Mary Jane*, I would have had those same shots in my possession the last forty-five years. Amazing!"

"Now that it's all over, for good, let's have a cold beer to celebrate," MacDonald said.

"There's one other thing," Cameron went on.

"What now?"

"The cultural shock on these guys if and when they reach the States will be tremendous. How about Crosby, for example, the radar operator? In 1945, he was married. The last time I heard his wife was alive. My wife and I exchanged Christmas cards with her. She and Mark were childhood sweethearts from a small town outside Omaha. She still lives there with her second husband. They had four kids. If Mark should meet up with her, it would be catastrophic for the both of them. The other crewmembers have brothers and sisters. What if–"

"We've thought of that already," MacDonald assured the general. "I'm sure the crew will not want to jeopardize their unique situation. If we send them back to the States under assumed names they will face orders to stay away from family and friends. They will just have to cope. But they do have age on their side. They can start all over again. Make new friends, get married, start a family."

Cameron laughed lightly. "I forgot about their ages. Do you really think it'll work?"

"What else can we do? We can't send them back to 1945."

"No, I guess not. Although you did try at gunpoint."

In a separate room, Les and Robert stood facing each other.

"I'm really proud of you, son."

Les was surprised. "You are?"

"Of course I am. When I saw your fighter up close on the carrier deck, I suddenly realized that was *your* fighter. Commodore Prentice thinks very highly of you. He told me that it took guts to turn away from the *Mary Jane*, knowing it would drop a nuclear bomb on David and Kyoto."

Les forced a grin. "I had my orders."

"I feel badly for how I treated you. My silent treatments. I've had to live with the *Mary Jane* and her disappearance since the war. As crew chief, I felt responsible. I thought for sure they had been shot down. They were my friends. I hated the war. I hated the Japs. I still do. They started the war. Because of them, many of my friends never came back. I just wanted to do my job and go home. It was a difficult time. After all these years, we know what happened to the *Mary Jane*. Finally!"

"Dad, are you proud of David, too?"

Robert took several seconds to answer. "That's something I'm going to have to work on."

"Let's face it, dad. David lives in Japan and may even marry a Japanese girl. I hope you'll accept her into the family as graciously as you did Gail." Les put his hand on his father's shoulder. "When you see David and his girlfriend, just turn on the old Robert Shilling charm. Gail thinks you're the best and can do no wrong."

* * * *

178

Back in the other room, MacDonald had brought in cold beer for everyone.

Nevin Brown finished his first. "Quite the cans. Kinda flimsy. Light beer, huh? By the way, colonel, I picked up a Jap radio station. It was playing the strangest song I ever heard. A band called Haley's Comet or something like that."

"You mean Bill Haley and the Comets," Les said.

"Yeah, that's them. *Rock Around the Clock*. A bouncy arrangement. Is that the kinda music they play now?"

Les grinned. "Not really. That song is a golden oldie, as we call them. It's over thirty years old."

"So what do people my age listen to in 1990?"

"Well. . ." Les wondered how he'd answer that. Where would he begin? *Michael Jackson. Madonna. Phil Collins. MC Hammer. The Rolling Stones.* "You'll have some catching up to do in that department. Maybe you should start with Elvis Presley. . . then take it from there."

Les, Cameron, Tiger, MacDonald, and Robert all laughed.

"Now, wait a damn minute here," Mark Crosby cut in. "Maybe some of you guys can laugh off these changes and have a good time talking about. . . these movies and these fancy beer cans and those crazy songs. . . and Elvis whoever-he-is. But what about me? Hell, I'm a married man. I got a wife to go home to."

"Not any more you don't," Cameron answered stiffly, stepping forward. "Dini remarried in 1947."

Crosby shook his head. "1947? I don't get this–"

"Our family has been exchanging Christmas cards with her and her husband for years."

"I'm back now! I'm back! I'm going home to Omaha."

"No you're not. Sergeant Mark Crosby, radar operator, does not exist. To you, you've only been gone a year or so. But to your wife. . . well, it's been forty-five years. What do you hope to accomplish? Dini's almost seventy. You're, let's see–"

"Twenty-five," Crosby fired away.

"You'd destroy her."

Clayton approached Crosby.

"Face the facts, Mark. We were all reported missing in action. Dini's not your wife. Mary Jane isn't my girl any longer, either, wherever she

179

may be. We're stuck. We're all in the same boat, Mark. Let's make the best of it."

"I told you before, the navy will look after you, men," MacDonald informed them. "Hang in there. We'll get you back into society."

Crosby fumbled in his front pocket. He lit a cigarette and puffed, his hands shaking. "This is ridiculous."

Twenty

Kyoto

David, Toshika, and Edna stood in the busy arrival area at the airport, waiting for the plane carrying Robert, Les, and his family to land.

On the screen above them, David saw their flight number flash ARR—arrival. In a few minutes, the entire Shilling family would be together again. Les, Gail, and the kids came into view first, waving as they came down the escalator to a glassed-in open area that separated them from the onlookers. The automatic door opened and Gail ran through first.

She hugged her brother-in-law. "David! You look great. A little heavier, but great."

"Thanks."

"You must be Toshika." Gail shook her hand. "I hear you're almost hitched. Congratulations. Oh hell, it's wonderful!" She hugged her.

David introduced Toshika to Les and the kids, then asked, "Where's pop?"

Les cleared his throat. "He's stalling. He sat at the tail, all by himself. He hasn't been talking much these last few days."

Finally, after several minutes, the group saw Robert, his head down until he reached the automatic door at the bottom.

"Brace yourself," Les whispered to David and Toshika.

"Hi, dad," David said, once the door opened. He put his hand out. Robert ignored the gesture and instead hugged his son. The two embraced.

"Dad," David said, pulling away, "I'd like you to meet my fiancée, Toshika Ushida."

Robert's eyes showed no emotion. He stood for a long time staring at her. Forty years of prejudice ran cold through his body. Looking into Toshika's brown eyes, he could see the faces of his buddies who had never returned from the war that the Japanese started. He saw a panoramic view of North Field, Tinian, B-29 after B-29 on the tarmacs. He saw himself twisting and tugging with a wrench, laboring away in the heat on one of *Mary Jane*'s engines. Robert was at a crossroad now. He could continue to hate the Japanese for starting the war or he could accept Toshika as one of the family.

Robert sighed and opened his arms. Toshika, tears in her eyes, embraced her future father-in-law. Robert looked into her eyes and said, "You are very pretty, young lady."

"Thank you."

"I've been doing a lot of thinking the last few days. It's going to take me some time to accept this arrangement, but I have to think of your futures. Times are different now. David has probably told you about me. I'm willing to change. I want us all to have a good time. I hope that in the next few days you'll show me all you can of your city. That's if you want to be caught with some crusty old goat."

Toshika wiped her tears. "Of course. . . *dad*."

Robert laughed out loud. "This may be tough for you, too."

"Let's get you all back to my place," David said, clapping his hands. "Toshika and I are on holidays for two weeks, so we're at your service. We're going to paint the town red!"

"Oh, no," Robert said. "Not another Tinian blowout. I'm not twenty anymore."